CZECH EXTREME

EDITORS

Edward Lee, Honza Vojtíšek, and Lisa Tone

Madness Heart Press
2006 Idlewilde Run Dr.
Austin, Texas 78744

Cover by John Baltisberger
Cover photography by Dennis Trevisan, Comfreak and Eilane
    Meyer
Interior Layout by Lori Michelle
    www.TheAuthorsAlley.com

For more information, address:
    john@madnessheart.press

www.madnessheart.press

TABLE OF CONTENTS

INTRODUCTION

DON'T GET ME WRONG; I'm an American and I'm damn proud to be. I think the USA is the greatest country on earth and has the best of everything . . . but of course, most anyone will probably think the same thing about their own countries. Not too long ago, I had the opportunity to travel multiple times to Poland and Germany; plus, in the late '70s, I served in the US Army and was stationed in what was then known as "West" Germany. So, be it recently or be it forty-plus years ago, I've been able to witness first hand the differences between America and Europe. And I can tell you now—with all due respect to the U.S. of A.—America doesn't have the best of everything, not by a long shot. Europe's got better food, better roads, better schools—oh, and lower crime across the board. Go to a McDonald's in Poland or Germany and you'll find that it's ten times better than McDonald's in America. Why? Higher quality ingredients. Better beef, better lettuce, better buns, etc. No antibiotics or steroids in the hamburger meat. Roads in Europe are examples of engineering perfection; in America, they're full of potholes ten years after they're built, or sooner. Why? Because in America, the road builder with the lowest bid always gets the job. Lowest bid equals lowest quality. Duh.

Ah, but the purpose of this introduction is not to highlight Europe's excellences over the US. (And to be fair, we've got our share of excellences here as well, just shitty fast food.)

Now let's talk about traditions of supernatural folklore. In America, the supply is pretty scant when compared to that of Europe. Europe is the seat of Western Civilization, the home of big cities with big populations going back thousands of years; while "America," as we know it, isn't even 500 years old. Before North America was colonized, the only "ghost stories" were sporadic tales handed down word-of-mouth from the Native Americans who've lived here, we're told, since the end of the last Ice Age, some 11,000 years ago. But people didn't live long back then, so there was never a big population of Native Americans. In 1620, for instance, it's estimated that less than 3000 Native Americans lived in the area that is now Massachusetts. Now these great folks have some great supernatural tales to tell—the Windigo comes first to mind—but it's not a very deep well. Europe, on the other hand, with active civilizations going back millennia, is neck deep in such traditions. Hence, it can be said that what eventually would evolve into the Modern Horror Genre were influences that migrated from Europe. The Czech Republic is a great example of a place that's teeming with diverse and terrifying folklore, a country that, hands down, has better and more great ghost stories than the US. Like Houska Castle, a medieval fortification said to be built right on top of the Gate to Hell! If you listen closely, you can hear the screams of the damned. Cool! Then there's the One-Armed Thief. See, long ago, some poor bastard broke into St. James the Greater Church and tried to steal the gold chalice, and it's said that St. Mary Herself caught him and TORE HIS ARM OFF. Ouch! Whether you believe it or not, that same mummified arm still hangs in the vestibule of the church. Don't believe me? Google it! There are pix! Perhaps the most famous Czech legend is one that's always enthralled me: The Golem of Prague. In the 1500s, the Jews of Prague were mercilessly persecuted by the emperor's soldiers, so the rabbi of the town used ancient Jewish mysticism to make a golem—a giant monster composed of riverbed clay— and this golem became a minister of vengeance and attacked the enemies of the Jews. Well, I probably don't need to tell you that the golem tore the hell out of the emperor's troops and almost got its hands on the emperor himself until the rabbi deactivated the monster and stashed its body in the attic of the Old New Synagogue. Google it. That synagogue is still there, but they won't let anyone up in the attic. Gee, I wonder why?

Anyway, what I'm getting to is the observation that much of the horror genre—that wonderful pie wedge of entertainment which we're talking about— is not only influenced by Europe but it's also appreciated by Europe today just as it's appreciated in America. For some reason, however, the majority of modern horror fiction seems to be produced by authors in the United States . . . or at least until now. Starting in the '90s, horror fiction in the US began to branch out and subdivide into different types of horror, and one of those types is Extreme Horror, and now we're seeing that spillover into Europe, where

Edward Lee

I'm happy to say that a whole new wave of writers are trying their hand at Extreme Horror of their own. There are movements popping up everywhere, Germany, Poland, Italy—ah, and also the Czech Republic.

Hence, here is the book you now hold in your hands, a collection of extreme horror stories written by an exciting crop of professional Czech authors and screenwriters. (The only story here not written by a Czech is mine.) It has been my pleasure to work on this project with co-editor Honza Vojtíšek, who solicited the authors, compiled the stories, and had them translated into English. So, he and I both thank you for giving this book a look. For me, it has been a captivating prospect indeed to see how authors of another country perceive and contribute to the extreme horror movement, and I hope you enjoy these stories as much as I did.

EDWARD LEE
author of *City Infernal* and *White Trash Gothic*

N

A FEW WORDS ABOUT LITERARY HORROR IN THE CZECH REPUBLIC.

THE HISTORY OF HORROR stories in the Czech lands goes back to legends, fairy tales, and so-called shopkeeper's songs performed at markets and fairs. They began to form and appear more significantly in literature in the second half of the 19th century in the form of dark to harsh poetic ballads and short stories. The most prominent author of haunting ballads to this day is the historian, archivist, and collector Karel Jaromír Erben, who has collected several haunting Czech stories. In the middle of the 19th century, his poetic collection of haunting and often brutal ballads Kytice z pověstí národních (Bouquet of National Legends, 1853, extended, supplemented edition 1861) was published, which is still taught about schools. Many more well-known and unknown authors have devoted themselves to haunting ballads, including one of the most famous and revered Czech writers, Božena Němcová, and her novel Babička (Grandmother), which is considered as a national treasure.

Ballads often reflected a more tragic and darker form of real life, whether it was drowning unwanted newborns in rivers, digging bones from graves by the hungry poor, cruelty and irreconcilability of lords, etc. Their next topic was meeting ghosts or their revenge for cruel and often bloody deaths. Unfortunately, many of these authors and their poems have fallen into oblivion. In short stories and novels, the spooky stories were devoted to the occult, the spooky, dreamy, or abstract novel to the visitor, the contemporary mysterious atmosphere with the necessary hopelessly realistic explanation of everything (the film called Sivooký Démon (Dove-grey Eyed Demon, 1873) by Jakub Arbes's romanetto).

To a certain extent, it was also literature from abroad. However, in some cases, it is not possible to speak directly of translations. At times, it was more of a (very) free retelling of the original story by a Czech author with his considerable authorial contribution, when he even added passages devised by himself.

On a darker and more serious level, a significant element of Czech horror comes to the foreground, which is the psychological side of horror or a mystical touch—for example, the short story Vampýr (The Vampire, 1871) by Jan Neruda. However, there are also some brutal body horror pieces: Genius Ohava (Genius Ugly, 1929) by Methodius Havlíček Tišnovský or Kosoručka (The Scythe-handed, 1869) by the already mentioned K. J. Erben. It is also worth mentioning Václav Rodomil Kramerius with his short story Železná košile (Iron Shirt, 1831), where he overtook "The Pit and The Pendulum" by E. A. Poe for 11 years.

At the turn of the 19th and the beginning of the

20th century, darker novels and short stories came into play, often inspired by the genius of places of domestic realities, their authors being of non-Czech origin—e.g., Gustav Meyrink's Golem (Der Golem, 1915) or some short stories by Franz Kafka. There are still occult stories in the course, the space is given more adventurous so-called bloody novels, connecting roughness and ruthlessness with fun, criminal, and thriller elements.

After the establishment of an independent Czechoslovakia, during the so-called First Republic, a relatively strong base of horror authors was formed, profiling literary horror in many different directions. There were certain vibes of Lovecraftian cosmic horror in the work of occultist Emanuel Lešehrad, mysteries of South African witchcraft from aristocracy-obsessed and Nazism-admirer Felix Achille de la Cámara (his real name was Felix Emil Josef Karel Cammra) or Japanese-influenced (way before it was cool) and inspired horrors by Joe Hloucha (e.g., short story about a long-haired ghost of a woman named O-Jiva-Inari-Daimiodin from 1920).

The psychological dimension of domestic horror was probably most pronounced in Jaroslav Havlíček's darkly depressing novel Neviditelný (The Invisible, 1937), about a mentally disturbed uncle (suffering from the idea that he is invisible) in the family of a certain factory owner. The story of the last week before the first menstrual period of the young girl Valerie a týden divů (Valerie and the week of wonders, 1932) of Vítězslav Nezval, who underwent an award-winning film adaptation in the 1970s, took an abstractly allegorical formula.

Honza Vojtíšek

After World War II, the Communist Party came to power in Czechoslovakia in 1948, and in terms of horror stories, for many years, the hard-to-reach cover fell on domestic horror. Horror, for its supernatural and often (non) human cruel nature, did not conform to Marx-Leninist materialist (and propagated humanist) doctrine. On the one hand, Czech and Slovak readers were deprived of the world's most basic horror works for four decades (Stephen King's novels did not appear in Czech until the early 1990s; Shirley Jackson's The Haunting of Hill House was not published in Czech until 2015) or even complete knowledge of many names from the modern history of literary horror. On the other hand, when some horror stories hit the police of Czech bookstores, it was mostly quality work.

The great promoter of horror literature in socialist Czechoslovakia in the late 1960s was the translator and editor Tomáš Korbař, who translated, for example, Dracula (Bram Stoker) and Frankenstein (Mary Shelley Wollstonecraft). Above all, however, in 1967, he managed to push into the publishing plan of the Mladá Fronta publishing house the still groundbreaking and awarded anthology of Anglo-American horror short stories Tichá hrůza (Silent Terror), which laid the foundation for modern horror in socialist Czechoslovakia. For many fans of literary horror, this is the unsurpassed and best horror book published in the Czech language. It contains now-classic short stories such as Call Him Demon (Henry Kuttner), The Birds (Daphne du Maurier), The Small Assassin (Ray Bradbury), or The Specialty of the House (Stanley Ellin). The last one mentioned also got a TV adaptation in the early 1990s. Tichá hrůza was also lucky enough to be printed in several editions (1970, 2008, 2016). The second anthology edited by Korbař is the vampire anthology Rej upírů (Swirl of vampires, 1970), which contains mainly older vampire stories. This book also received newer editions (2005, 2015). An anthology named Opičí tlapka (Monkey´s Paw) was compiled from Korbař's translation estate in 2009, named after the famous short story by W. W. Jacobs.

Korbař's literary activity opened the door to other (mostly translated) anthologies of horror short stories: Fantastické povídky (Fantastic Short Stories, 1968), Stráž u mrtvého (The Watcher by the Dead, 1969) or the second most distinctive and significant anthology of its time, Lupiči mrtvol (The Body Snatcher, 1970), in which Czech readers were able to meet the work of Howard Phillips Lovecraft (specifically the short story The Terrible Old Man) for the first time. Occasionally, short stories by domestic authors (mostly from the turn of the 19th and 20th centuries) were rarely included in anthologies created by domestic editors. The horror stories of that time, not only by domestic authors, were pushed here and there into various sci-fi anthologies, yearbooks, and selections. Edgar Allan Poe has become an absolute classic, but selections and collections by authors such as Joseph Sheridan Le Fanu, Nathaniel Hawthorne, and Ray Bradbury have also appeared.

From the domestic works of the post-war period until the fall of socialism in November 1989, it is worth mentioning the dark psychological horror about the complete disintegration of the human mind in the novel named Spalovač mrtvol (The Cremator, 1967) by Ladislav Fuks and the short story Upír LTD (Vampire LTD, 1962) by Josef Nesvadba about a car driving on human blood. Both pieces were adapted into the film by probably the most prominent Czech horror director, Juraj Herz (The Cremator, 1968 and Ferat Vampire, 1981). Another significant contribution to domestic horror was the collection of short stories by Miloslav Švandrlík, Drákulův švagr (Dracula's brother-in-law, 1970). Švandrlík became famous mainly as a humorist, but he was a great lover of the horror genre and wrote 300 horror short stories during his lifetime. His stories were marked by strong skepticism (Švandrlík believed in supernatural and occult practices and liked to ridicule and "take revenge" on skeptics through his short stories) and black, ironic, often mischievous humor. Nevertheless, he could be freezingly harsh in his stories. Several short stories from this collection were adapted for the television series of the same name in the mid-1990s. After the fall of socialism, practically all of his horror work was published in several dozen different book selections.

The boom in horror literature in the Czech Republic came after the fall of the socialist regime and the loss of power of the Communist Party in November 1989. In the early 1990s, a lot of horror literature piled up on the shelves of bookshops and newsstands, although several basic works of horror literature are still missing in the Czech translation up today. Stephen King quickly gained popularity with readers (even though his first translations were not received very positively), followed by Clive Barker,

Dean R. Koontz, and, over time, Howard Phillips Lovecraft. The books of James Herbert, Peter James, Anne Rice, and two novels by Graham Masterton appeared in a short time. Already proven and recognized names from the West were entering the viewfinder. R. L. Stine opened the gates to the world of horror for younger readers. Ivan Adamovič, a reporter, translator, and editor who did a great job in foreign horror, first edited two volumes of Půlnoční stíny (Midnight Shadows, 1991 & 1992) book anthology in the early 1990s to compile in 1997 the ultimate anthology of the Anglo-American horror short stories of the genre Hlas krve (The Voice of Blood, 1997), probably the second most fundamental and most basic horror short storybook published in Czech.

The door also opened to domestic horror. In the early 1990s, domestic authors and publishers tried to take advantage of the free entry of the new genre and interest in it. Domestic authors wrote and published under foreign (English and American) sounding pseudonyms (e.g., the author of crime and biographical books Heda Bartíková published several horror short stories and collections under the name Hedy Bartley). Fantastic magazines appeared here and there, giving space to horror (Nemesis, Ducháček, Ikarie - today XB-1, which until recently devoted every October issue to pure horror, later Pevnost magazine), as well as attempts at pure horror magazines. In 1998, two issues of the very nice magazine Horror were published, the magazine Král Horror (published first on paper, later electronically) focused purely on domestic short stories. Eventually, its publication was transformed into a series of horror anthologies, Antologie českého hororu (The Anthology of Czech Horror, 2011-2017). Since 2012, the e-magazine Howard has been published regularly every quarter of the year.

In a more widespread and generally acceptable version, domestic horror was combined with other genres (sci-fi, fantasy, action, crime). The most prominent domestic names of the 1990s and early new centuries include Svatopluk Doseděl (several short story collections, the novel Bestseller (2005)), Jenny Nowak, who focuses mainly on vampire and werewolf themes, and Petra Neomillnerová, who created an action series about vampires, with which she got beyond the borders of the Czech Republic. At the beginning of the new millennium, the author Anna Šochová also made a significant contribution to domestic horror with her emotionally raw stories from the Czech-German border. Other generally fantastic authors such as Jiří W. Procházka, Františka Vrbenská or Petra Slováková sometimes engage in horror.

A lot of work for the Czech horror and its support was done by the editor Antonín KK Kudláč, who seems to be responsible for the first explicitly horror anthology of modern domestic horror 2004: Český horor (2004: The Czech Horror, 2003), which he eventually supplemented with another anthology of the domestic horror, Cáry rubáše (Tatters of a shroud, 2011). Horror books, even those by domestic authors (Jenny Nowak, Kristina Haidingerová, Jiří Šedý), appeared in the edition plan of the Netopejr publishing house.

More and more names are appearing in today's domestic horror. Pavel Renčín wrote a raw horror novel inspired by real events from the border of socialist Czechoslovakia Vězněná (Imprisoned, 2015), he also wrote a collection of short stories, Beton, kosti a sny (Concrete, Bones and Dreams, 2009). Kristina Haidingerová, a great promoter of the horror genre, editor of a series of domestic horror anthologies or poetry anthologies, and organizer of the HorrorCon, dedicated her (so far) duology Ti nepohřbení (Those Unburied, 2015), Děti Raumy (The Children of Rauma, 2019) and also in several related short stories to the poetically atmospheric horror (mainly in a vampire robe) and the so-called Violets. Petr Boček follows in the footsteps of Miloslav Švandrlík, whose short stories and novels combine pure horror with chilling black and ironic humor. Many collections and novels by domestic authors are still published in an underground way and on their own.

Extreme horror entered the Czech Republic in the early 1990s through the early work of Clive Barker (Hellbound Heart, Books of Blood, The Great and Secret Show) and two translated volumes from a series of anthologies of erotic horrors Hot Blood (Hot Blood in 1996 and Hotter Blood in 1997). Only later, after 2010, did translations of Richard Laymon's books (The Cellar in 2009, The Traveling Vampire Show and One Rainy Night in 2010, Funland in 2012) appear, and after 30 years did Czech readers finally see Off Season: The Unexpurgated Edition (2011) by Jack Ketchum. The latter quickly gained fans in the Czech Republic, and translations of his other books soon followed. A few years later, the books of Carlton

Honza Vojtíšek

Mellick III (the first Czech translation in Howard magazine in 2014, his books regularly since 2018) or Edward Lee (Trolley No. 1852 in 2019) were published, and in 2021, an extreme horror novel, Suffer the Flesh by Monica J. O'Rourke, was published by Golden Dog. Since 2019, books by the Slovak author Mark E. Pocha have also been published in the Czech Republic, which revel in bizarreness, brutality, and explicit violence. Foreign and domestic extreme horror is regularly given space through short stories in the electronic horror magazine Howard (the first was the translation of Edward Lee's work into Czech in 2012). At the turn of the millennium, the extreme horror at home was given a unique space in the generally fantastic short story competition Ježíšku, já chci plamenomet (Santa, I Want a Flamethrower), whose winning and interesting short stories appeared in regularly published anthologies of the same name. The screenwriter, director, and writer Roman Vojkůvka, who published his own collection Řezničina (The Butchery) in 2011 after several magazine publications, made a significant impact on Czech extreme horror. Miroslav Pech entered the genre to the brink of hardcore horror with the raw social novel Mainstream (2018), which was first published in Poland, then at home in the Czech Republic. He also strums the rougher, rawer, and more extreme string in some of his short stories. Recently, the work of Petr Boček, as well as the work of the author of this preface, has become increasingly resorted to extreme and bizarre levels. However, the Czech horror is still waiting for the distinctive and more established face of the extreme offshoot.

Horror in general, and the domestic one in particular, was until recently (and still is) considered the last in the fantastic trio of science fiction, fantasy, and horror. He is still considered by many to be an integral part of fantasy and is denied an independent and distinctive status. Czech horror did not have many ways and means to hone its qualities and show them to the public. He didn't get enough space both on the shelves of bookstores and on the pages of magazines and programs of fantastic cones. For so long, the domestic horror plunged into only the musty and dusty waters of the underground. Only in recent years can we see a pleasant improvement. More authors, more domestic books, more publishers focused partly or completely on the horror genre. This is due to the work of several ardent individuals and, more recently, the growth of small genre publishers giving space not only to foreign authors unknown in the Czech Republic but also to domestic male and female authors. Large publishing houses include publishing divisions (e.g., Phobos) dedicated to foreign horror or specific editions. E.g., Volvox Globator published the edition of Alrúna, which published the old and historical foundations of the horror and mystery (Sheridan Le Fanu, August Derleth & H. P. Lovecraft, Arthur Machen, E. T. A. Hoffmann, Jules Janin).

Smaller publishing houses began to devote themselves significantly to horror. In addition to fantasy and sci-fi books, Gnóm brought novels and short stories by Philip Fracassi, Brian Evenson, and Laird Barron. Since 2022, Gnóm has been preparing a horror edition of Horla. Significant space for Czech readers unknown to foreigners (the first Czech book translations Mort Castle, Monica J. O'Rourke, Owl Goingback) and domestic horror authors (e.g., Petr Boček, Veronika Fiedlerová, Jiří Sivok, Ludmila Svozilová) gives the genre publishing house Golden Dog, whose owner Martin Štefko himself wrote several horror novels and short stories. One of the main goals of Golden Dog is to support Czech horror. The pure horror publishing house, which publishes mainly foreign translations, is Carcosa (Carlton Mellick III, John Everson, Edward Lee, Clive Barker, S. T. Joshi). And recently, Medusa publisher came out with the first translated book.

Czech horror and horror in the Czech Republic finally, after years of being neglected and overlooked, get the word out and get its share of attention. Not only in the cultural and social space (cons, meetings with authors, author's readings, etc.), but also in the press and on the internet. And that's only good because Czech horror has something to say and show. After all, now you can see for yourself . . .

Honza Vojtíšek
October 8, 2021

A BROTHEL OF YOUR DREAMS

Roman Vojkůvka

translated by Karolína Svěcená

EMIL HAD A birthday tomorrow, and Artur prepared a present for him.

They had known each other only for a few weeks, but from the beginning, they understood each other as if they were old friends. The interest in perverted sex brought them so close that even that first evening, when they had accidentally talked at the bar, they raped a young girl together in the park, then kicked her and finally, cut her face with a broken bottle. There was a manly bond between them, nothing "gay," as Emil would say, just a friendship with a big fucking F.

On Emil's birthday, they had a few beers in the Crooked Man's Pub and looked at the women who were there. They were wondering what to do with them, to have them in a damp, windowless cellar room with a toolbox full of sharp, pointed, and otherwise fun items.

After finishing their sixth beer, Artur said, "It's time for a birthday surprise."

Roman Vojkůvka

Emil knew it wouldn't be a twenty-nine-candle cake, nor a boring and absurdly high-priced stripper in which you couldn't even put your finger without paying extra. He knew it would be worth it. He paid for both.

They walked through alleys he did not know, although he had lived in this city since childhood. Dirty nooks and crannies alternated with urine-smelling underpasses, inscriptions on the walls with humor of the coarsest grain and a quantum of used syringes on the ground. They walked around the peeling houses, covered with mold like sea reefs, met strange individuals whose eyes had little to do with humans, and waded through piles of rubbish as a baby from the womb penetrates the great unknown world. Emil felt the same way. He went into the unknown too, and Artur was the one he trusted infinitely, just as a little human being naturally trusts his mother.

In the last underpass was a peeling sheet metal door without a handle, with a rusty patina and the large red letters "ANT TO FUC", which were part of an inscription that began before and ended behind this entrance.

"We're here," Artur said, pulling out his cell phone. He rang someone and hid his cell phone back in his pocket. He pulled out a pack of cigarettes and knocked out two, one for himself and the other for his friend. As soon as they lit, the door slammed open. Behind them, a large fat guy in a white T-shirt with the words "I love life" in Portuguese appeared—he just didn't know it; he couldn't speak Portuguese, and no one translated it for him.

"Hello, Robert," Artur said.

"Hi," Emil added, though he had never seen the man in his life.

Robert didn't look very friendly. Instead of answering the greeting, he studied Emil for a moment. He felt that something was wrong with him. When he finally realized what, he snapped at Artur, "Why doesn't he have a blindfold? Don't you fucking know the rules?"

Emil was a little uncertain.

"He is a friend. I trust him," Artur said calmly. He blew the smoke casually in front of him and shrouded Robert's "I Love Life" in a dirty cigarette mist.

"FRIEND?" Robert repeated emphatically.

"I'm saying that, FRIEND."

Robert nodded and let them in. Both guests entered, and when the corpulent doorman closed the door behind them with a loud creak, red letters W and K on the walls around the door became part of one sentence again.

He didn't go downstairs with them. No need, Artur knew it as well as his own kitchen and was a great guide. Maybe better than his kitchen. He never enjoyed cooking very much.

As they descended the last step to the concrete plane, Artur stopped. He turned to his companion and looked solemn. It was clear to Emil that something like a birthday speech would come. Of course, it came.

"My friend," Artur began, and after a short pause, he continued.

"You are in the place you have dreamed of all your life, in the place where your most perverted erotic dreams can come true, where the women from your imagination are real and let you really, really do whatever you want. Just choose."

He looked into Emil's eyes. He smiled when he was sure he saw the expectations and tension he was looking for.

"Ready?"

"Ready."

They passed a lot of doors, and Artur opened them all to Emil's eager eyes. They saw a girl with lots of breasts all over her body, a woman who had no legs or arms, only a torso and head available to desirable customers, another with four arms and two vaginas, another with two heads, then a female body without a head, artificially kept in operation, siamese twins with whole bodies or divided in a way that something important was missing. Barely adult girls and old women with living rotting bodies, human females with faces and bodies so mutilated that even Cronenberg wouldn't dream of it in his wildest dreams, bizarre beauties serving their bodies for the pleasures of "human" beings who couldn't be aroused by natural human beauty anymore. And Emil liked it all so much. He felt like he was in a paradise he had created in his perverted brain. He longed to taste all those obscurely beautiful women, enter their bodies, and satisfy his perverted lust.

And Artur spoke and talked, explained and clarified . . .

" . . . Unrecognized artists, bankrupt scientists, and plastic surgeons without a license are working for us. Some even have a license; it just seems to them that it pays more to make monsters out of the beauties than vice versa. I think there is something about it . . . "

He had a story for amusement or reflection for each of those doors.

"This girl came here voluntarily, where else to get a job with a cunt under her chin. Maybe she should have become model showing the turtlenecks . . . but she probably didn't think of that . . . "

At one point, he allowed Emil to come closer.

"Don't worry about her, she won't spit that far. No, she doesn't speak, she has no tongue . . . "

Then the excursion ended, and Artur asked significantly, "Did you choose?"

Emil squinted in surprise.

"What the fuck did you expect it to be, an excursion to the zoo?" Artur chuckled. "Just choose one of them. It's your birthday, and I'm paying. "

"Thanks, man," Emil wanted to hug Artur. He wouldn't do it, of course. It would be too "gay."

"It's hard," he said at once, "they're all so wonderfully exciting."

"I know a woman with eight tits, just like a blow job from a girl with a cleft. But you only get to choose one. Only one of them will be your favorite. A girl you won't forget until death. The weirdest chick you've ever gotten into. "

Emil smiled.

"I see you have chosen."

Emil nodded.

He chose a creature with five vaginas, two on the outside of the thighs and two on the hips, the original one wired in six places and dripping with drops of bloody pus between its rusty seams. The woman herself hung by her hands from the ceiling so that the customer could caress the breasts she had transplanted on her back while standing. In place of the original ones, there were deep red scars on the flat chest.

Artur closed the door, and Emil was left alone with his chosen one. As he admired her with a gaze, she watched him indifferently. She didn't speak, her wired mouth wouldn't allow it. Emil understood that this going to be without kissing.

Everything about her aroused him. The non-traditional placement of some parts, the improvement and multiplication of erotic areas, and even the remains of needle pricks on the hands and feet. He came closer and began to touch her, first gently, then harder. She didn't protest. He tried to give her a few punches. It made funny claps. She didn't even make a sound. He realized he could do anything. Absolutely anything.

He chose a vagina on her left thigh. When he entered her and crushed her breasts on her back with his hands, he knew he really wouldn't forget this. His demented pleasure increased a thousandfold. And then he just got carried away and fell and fell (. . . and fell . . .) somewhere into the unknown as the damp dark world around him ceased to exist. Suddenly, it was pitch dark. Emil had never known anything like this.

He woke up in a few weeks. His whole body ached because plastic surgeons had created four artificial vaginas and two other anal openings on his body, all intentionally kept unhealed. His penis was removed, leaving only his testicles. One of the vaginas was on the abdomen, another on the back. The other two where his eyes used to be. That's why he couldn't see the six scantily clad businessmen who came to enjoy what they paid for. But he heard them well and understood what would happen. They started pushing something into him from all sides. They laughed, sighed, and shouted the vulgar insults at him. He shouted in horror. He screamed because he could. Customers wanted it that way.

CAMEL TOE

Honza Vojtíšek

translated by Karolína Svěcená

KAREL HAD LONG considered himself a happy man. Mainly because he managed to combine pleasant with useful. He realized at an early age that he liked (much) older women. And when he later spent the night with an elderly lady and the next morning she offered him money for it, he just smiled, took it, and a plan was born in his head. His work as a gigolo for a very specific clientele brought him not only money but also the pleasure and satisfaction of his lust. It was great. He didn't even have to offer or advertise himself, the satisfied ladies were passing on his number like a recipe for a sweet dessert. He could not complain about lack of work. Some of the ladies were very generous beyond his usual price, but they were all nice. What was gratifying about all this, however, was the fact that gerontophilia was practically completely overshadowed by the more pronounced and, in a way, more grateful pedophilia on the public witch hunt.

Karel was simply satisfied, happy, and secure.

However, when he entered a cottage in a remote cottage settlement where a client was already waiting to spend a night with him, it occurred to him that this old lady already belonged to the rank of hard-earned money. Because this was too much for him.

It didn't happen often, but sometime he met clients outside their place of residence. He never asked the reason because he knew it and it did not surprise him. Some women wanted to maintain discretion at the most effective level possible. He was therefore used to sunken hotels, rest houses, or cottage settlements.

"Karel Karafiát," he introduced himself and offered her his hand. He never invented a fake name. His real name was so stupid and ridiculous itself that no one could have thought it was real.

"Um," she snarled slightly like a cat, looking him over head to toe. "I like carnations." She gently trapped his palm in hers and stroked it.

"Libuše."

She must be over eighty. Karel couldn't get the idea out of his head. Not that it scared him, but he wondered if he had ever reached that high an age. She was really old, withered, shrunken. Proof that from some point on, the best ability to make yourself a pretty woman is insufficient. Although he could still see the spark in her eyes, he was especially vigilant, afraid to touch her so she wouldn't fall apart. He would have to be careful to ensure he pleased her, not hurt her.

Maybe she felt his embarrassment. She pulled a scuffed black-and-white photograph from her suit pocket and slipped it into his hand. "Maybe this will help you."

He looked at the photo. It was a young woman in a bikini posing on the seashore. She was pretty, with long straight hair, strong hips. Slightly protruding tummy, firm breasts. Today, only something similar to two withered scabs remained of them. Karel could appreciate the feminine beauty, but the girl in the photo was too young for him.

"You look nicer older," he said flatteringly, dropping the photo on the ground.

He walked close to her. He didn't come to talk.

"You would almost convince me." She smiled and took off her coat. "I have a nose for a lie."

When they were both in their underwear, he led her to the bed. She had smooth monochromatic linen. He liked it; he had to appreciate that she was aware that some extravagance would have a bizarre effect on her life-tired body. He was intrigued by how her panties were cut. They seemed to be hiding a single juicy and fleshy piece of the otherwise dry body. In their youth, they called it a camel toe and laughed at its wearers. Now he was quite happy about it.

In bed, while cuddling, all embarrassment subsided. She may be a few months older than he was used to, but it was still within the limits of his taste, lust, and excitement. Maybe it was true that certain things disappear when lying down.

They talked for a while, stroked, and looked at each other. When kissing (*She has a mustache, SHE HAS A MUSTACHE! For God's sake, nowadays?*) they took off the last pieces of clothing. He ran his palms over her wrinkled skin and felt the excitement rush down there. Libuše was not reserved at all. Thoughts of hard-earned money were now shyly shrinking somewhere in the corner in a room full of joyfully bouncing lust.

Her breasts . . . They just weren't there. Only leather folded in two places. The slightly protruding tummy from the photo was replaced by loosely crumpled paper. But he had to admit that she smelled good, so when he got his mouth down there, it was nicer than it seemed. He felt as if her fleshy vagina was reacting to his lips, as if it was kissing him back, and once or twice, he even heard the sweet clap that came out of her.

When they were really hot, tender, properly prepared, and in a firm embrace, he whispered in her ear the question of how she wished it. He was used to the fact that these women already have so much experience and know their bodies so well that they often have special wishes that satisfy them the most. Their suggestions did not seem strange or surprising to him, he had a few favourite spices that aroused him to the maximum, but he did not have the courage and, in fact, no desire to tell them to every woman with whom he shared a bed. But this was a little different, she had paid for it, and given her age and the associated sexual frequency, he expected similar wishes to be part of the evening. More than once, he was pleasantly surprised and even excited. For example, when he had fucked one old lady in the armpit, it was very pleasant. For both. When he urinated on the feet of another woman, it was at least strange. Just because of what it was doing to her. If he licked her all night, he wouldn't bring her to something like that, no matter how hard he tried.

Honza Vojtíšek

Libuše wanted to do it with his feet.

"You just stick your whole foot in there," she said. "Don't worry, I had it there to almost half the calf once. "

Karel, though surprised, had already done a lot of things, but not yet something like this. However, he was here to satisfy and fulfill her wishes. And so, he wasn't too embarrassed. He anointed his toes and his entire foot up above his ankle, pushed a chair over to the bed, sat down on it as comfortably as possible, and slipped in Libuše´s swollen labia with his toe.

He didn't expect it to be so pleasant for him. She accepted him without resistance, helpfully and warm. He twisted his foot a little and sent two more toes to visit.

Libuše sighed and opened even more. In a few moments, she accepted all the toes of Karel's foot. Her labia kissed his foot like the lips of a horny old virgin. She encouraged him several times, asking him to be more direct and emphatic.

He obeyed, pushing, and to his great surprise, Libuše´s vagina swallowed his foot above the ankle.

"Twist," Libuše breathed, her head bowed in excitement. Her body arched like a bow and vibrated slightly.

So he started twisting his foot carefully from side to side. She shuddered loudly. Her vagina clapped softly.

And then suddenly, it bit.

Karel felt something bite into his leg. Despite the layer of old, withered flesh, he heard a sharp crunch and found that he had lost control of his foot. It took an incredibly long time for him to scream in pain. He didn't have time for that. There was too much going on.

Libuše arched her back into a bridge.

Karel grabbed his calf just above where it had disappeared in Libuše´s vagina and tried to pull his leg out. It didn't work. On the contrary. He felt something pulling it inside. A trickle of blood flowed from the vagina, and Karel tried to convince himself that it was only because of it that the labia seemed to move.

Libuše´s back slammed against the bed. She spread her legs to an incredible angle. Her wrinkled belly began to swell and collapse like a bag sucking air in and out. To his horror, he found that it worked more like a pump. She began to pull him inside. There was another crunch, and the leg went into Libuše up to the knee. It was almost like a mechanical movement. Bite, pull in, and again.

He felt the pain take over and slowly displace the fear that was still on top. His muscles began to twitch, and he heard the muffled crack of his bones from the woman's abdomen. Blood rushed to his head. He foolishly grabbed the hope that the pressure would crack his head before it devoured him all.

The old woman's abdomen was still swelling like in a bizarre pregnancy, her labia absorbing more and more inches of Karel's shin. She sighed loudly and stroked her trembling fingers where her breasts had been several decades ago.

Karel, on the other hand, screamed. He began to scream continuously as his knee disappeared. And he stopped only when his crotch crunched loudly, and into the woman, behind her blackened labia (similar to ruffled raisins), disappeared his navel and a piece of strangely twisted other leg. His body must have fainted, mercifully. Or it finally died. Who knows . . .

It was slowly dawning when a young girl came out of the bathroom in the cabin. Her long straight hair flowed halfway down her back. Loose, brightly coloured T-shirt supported by firm, pointed breasts without a bra protruding forward. Long, seductively smooth legs coming out from under the miniskirt, finished with high stiletto heel boots. Distinctive makeup on a lovely face, a handbag over her shoulder, a softly rattling plastic bag in her hand.

She glanced around the darkened room and walked to the door. She stopped abruptly two meters away. Something stopped her. She bent her flawless knees and bent down to pick up a black-and-white photograph from the floor. She looked at herself appreciatively until her dark purple lips parted in a smile.

"Like looking in a mirror," she said confidently, slipping the photo into her purse. She would have to make a new one at the first opportunity. More contemporary.

She was reaching for the doorknob when she screamed aloud and quickly twisted. In a slight forward bend, she grabbed her stomach with her free hand. She had an unpleasant spasm. Painful pressure.

"Damn, one more," she sighed.

She dropped the plastic bag on the floor. With both hands, she slightly pulled up the miniskirt, parted her legs, and squatted as if she wanted to pee. She didn't have to bother with her panties, she wouldn't need them for a while.

She pursed her lips intently and pushed lightly. She released a quiet fart, but that was only a side effect. The real purpose was to spread the finely shaped pink labia, from the centre of which a shaft of a brightly bleached femur protruded. As it drove out and fell to the carpet with a soft thud, the girl breathed a sigh of relief.

She untied the plastic bag and threw the bone in with the others. She adjusted herself, left the key in the outside door, and left with the plastic bag in hand.

She threw him out somewhere along the way.

DOMINIK IS DIFFERENT

Miroslav Pech

translated by Karolína Svěcená

DOMINIK'S COLLEAGUE LIBOR has been suffering from strong flatulence since morning. Dominik doesn't mind. It suits him, and he likes it. He inconspicuously sniffs every time the office resonates with another fart. Dominik doesn't want Libor to think of something nor have any suspicions, shortly anything that would discredit Dominik.

"I have to shit," says Libor and gets up quickly.

When he leaves the room, Dominik rushes to the chair. He falls to his knees, pulls off the face mask, sinks his nose into the seat, and deeply absorbs the smell of musty and tangled fabric. It's fantastic. He hugs the chair as a lover and continues to sniff. Then the sound of doors opening and closing can be heard from the corridor. The upcoming steps follow. Dominik jumps up and runs to his table. He gets on the chair just as Libor enters the room. Dominik turns and looks at his colleague's swollen face strewn with fading red spots.

"Is it better?"

Libor shrugs. "Yes, a little."

"You probably ate something bad."

"Hmm." Libor sits down with a gasp, the chair slams under his weight, and he sighs. Dominik senses the smell of excrement from him. It's strong and hot, but not as much as it must be in the lavatory. Dominik wants more. He knows that this won't last him for very long.

On the way from work, he passes through the centre of Stone Trees, his home town. He is hot, so he sits on a bench in front of a shopping mall, where everything is closed except for grocery, and watches people. He is fascinated, as if he is seeing something like this for the first time. They are beautiful, all of them. He likes fat men and women the most, from whom a pleasant odor comes to him. Everyone is blowing farts; one would not even think how many people fart in just a minute. Dominik moves the face mask under his nose. He is like a dog, turning his head in all directions, face motionless with concentration and excitement in his eyes. He is alert, he is sniffing.

Soon, he has to get up and go somewhere where there is no such rumble, otherwise, he would go crazy. He could do something . . . something . . . that would cast a bad light on him. Something that the people would not understand. Not like he does. Because Dominik is different. That's right, he belongs to a different kind. He doesn't know exactly when it started—probably the day before, when he'd walked around the canal and fought the almost uncontrollable urge to pounce on it and bury his nose between the hatch grilles—but it doesn't matter.

Miroslav Pech

He comes to a bus stop—something tells him it's not exactly the best idea—and waits for the bus. That's not a good idea at all. He is different, he should not stand at the bus stop and take the bus, but it has already happened. The old woman next to him has a full gut. A young man nearby is just forming a massive load inside. That young man knows it or at least begins to suspect it. He treads nervously and taps on his cell phone. In an hour, a maximum of two, he will be sitting on a toilet. The old woman may not be able to make it, her inner clock is ticking louder and louder, and she is feeling anxious. She needs to get rid of the pressure, but if she drops just a little fart, only slightly opens the sphincter, she will have full bottoms.

When the bus arrives and its door slides open, passengers get out and pass gas. Heavy air pours out of the bus, mixing the smell of sweat, diseases, and full intestines. The young man with the cell phone gets on, the old woman doesn't. It's clear to her that she can't make it. She heads to a low building of public toilets. Dominik follows her. A sweaty woman sits inside and collects change. The old woman hands her a coin, takes a few pieces of toilet paper, and as soon as her sore legs allow, she hurries to the cabin. Dominik also takes his toilet allotment. However, instead of a place for gentlemen, he enters the next door. He listens carefully, but there is no one else except for him and the old woman. He enters the cabin next to her and locks the door. He lowers the toilet seat and sits on it. He listens to the old woman as she relaxes on a toilet seat and releases what has been relentlessly bothering her for so long. Dominik is like a fly slapped on a tiled wall, he has the face mask under his chin, ear pressed on a cold surface, and his nose pressed against the wall so hard that he is afraid that his nasal septum will burst.

He raises his head. The wall separating the cabins ends about half a meter below the ceiling. Dominik jumps up, grabs the edge, and pulls up. The old woman has her head back, so she is looking at Dominik with fear in her eyes.

"What are you doing?" Her voice trembles, while she's blindly trying to cover her thin, wrinkled legs.

Dominik lets go of the wall, unlocks the door, and runs out of the cabin. He puts on his face mask, walks past the woman behind the counter—she solves the crossword puzzle and doesn't even look up at him—and is back on the street. He accelerates until he finally runs, and the world around him is one big delicious slurry.

When he thinks that he's out of danger, he slows down. Dominik exhales, his heart stops pounding so fast. He walks along the river; the sun is just a hot glowing ball hanging in the cloudless sky, people exchanged jackets for T-shirts and blouses, men and boys pull out shorts, and the braver girls, miniskirts. Most of the benches are empty except one, where a man is resting. He has short black hair and apparently a home-made face mask over his mouth with a pattern resembling Native Americans. He presses his cell phone to his ear and talks cheerfully. He has a pram behind him. A child is lying in it, and Dominik feels that it's just pooping. He sneaks quietly to the pram and peers into it. The baby is sleeping. Dominik looks up at the man. He keeps talking on the phone and doesn't pay attention to anything else. Dominik uncovers the child and takes off its miniature sweatpants with embroidered teddy bears on its knees. He doesn't have to be a genius to know that the diaper is full. Not only does he see it, but he smells it above all. And the smell is so intense that his eyes are watering.

Dominik checks the man on the bench. Then he slides the face mask under his chin and unbuckles the baby's diaper. He looks at the thin dark yellow excrement. He digs his fingertip into it, lifts it to his face, and stabs it in the mouth as if licking chocolate. But children's feces taste much better. A million times better. Like the best chocolate Dominik ever had a chance to taste. No, he had never tasted it, it had never been made. The taste of feces exceeded all of Dominik's expectations. He grabs the diaper and burrows his mouth into it. He is so busy devouring and licking that sparse pile that he doesn't even notice the pair of children watching him in astonishment. When he licks the last thing, he grabs the waking child because this wasn't all. The child didn't push out the whole load. The man doesn't stop talking, he seems to be interpreting a politically incorrect joke. Dominik lifts it over his head so that the baby's buttocks are as close to his face as possible, then he opens his mouth and presses his thumbs against the baby's tummy. At that moment, the baby starts crying. And as soon as that happens, a couple of boys, whose presence Dominik will notice only now, shout. The child's father looks back and drops the cell phone.

"What the . . . ?" says the man.

Dominik looks nervously from man to child to the

boys, back to the child, and then to his father. He doesn't know who to look at first. The man is on his feet; Dominik knows that he will punch him at any moment and beat the shit out of him. But it won't happen. The man is so overwhelmed by what he sees that he can do nothing but a few incoherent sentences.

Dominik puts the crying baby back in the pram and covers it.

"I'm sorry," he says to the man. "I cannot help myself."

After those words, he runs around the shocked boys, puts a face mask over his stained lips, and runs.

When it's far enough away and no man in sight, he hides in the thick bush by the river. He lays on his back, pulls off the face mask, and licks the remnants of still wet excrement from his lips. Then he thinks of the cameras. At public toilets, at benches . . . He tries to calm down, they can't be everywhere. But Dominik knows that they are. The cameras are at every step, watching him, turning to him, aiming at him. *But I have a face mask*, he thinks, and perhaps for the first time, he's happy for it. *Thank God, the Devil, or a broken test tube in some secret underground lab, whatever everyone chooses, for the global coronavirus pandemic that makes people wear face masks.*

He sniffs, infallibly puts his hand behind him, grips the long dog poop, and calmly bites it. It's not like licking a baby's diaper, dry dog poop is not as fresh as warm diarrhea, of course, but he has to settle for what it is.

Before he goes home, Dominik collects and eats a

few more dog and cat excrements. He also discovers human ones, smelling of alcohol, old age, all sorts of diseases, the remains of dead parasites and their laid eggs. He drives away grazing flies, picks up some, and hides them in a bag leftover from a snack, others he leaves lying because he can't eat everything. Besides, shit lies everywhere and is free.

Dominik meditates on the couch with his beloved Enya playing from the headphones. He has listened to *Only Time* and now he is humming *Orinoco Flow*. There is a plate on his stomach with a pleasant-smelling pile of shit, and the world feels amazing. With Enya and enough food, he doesn't have to think about the disease, dying people, and doesn't have to worry about imminent dismissal from his job for redundancy. He no longer has to work; he doesn't need money for buying food from the shops because he came up with another and much better source. He still goes to work because he doesn't have much to do here and, well, he can buy an LP from Enya. He has several original CDs, but no LP so far. He can buy a gramophone and play the record. That's a great idea. Sometimes it happens to Dominik that he has a great idea. And this is one of those moments.

He devours another bite. His mouth, chin, and fingers are stained with feces. Dominik eats without cutlery because he likes to touch food and wants to be in direct contact with it. When the plate is empty, he takes a shower and pours hot water on himself. He doesn't want to wash away the odor, because it is no odor at all, but he can still think rationally. *More of a petty bourgeoisie*, Dominik thinks. He smiles bitterly. Surely, what would people say if they smelled him . . .

He squats, puts his hands underneath, forms a bowl with them, and pushes. A smooth, almost exemplary, slightly rounded cone slips out of his anus. Unfortunately, it was so long that it broke in half. Dominik can't resist and starts another course.

A week passes. Dominik still goes to work. In the evening, he takes an opaque plastic bag and goes out to collect shit, which he then consumes in the peace of home. It's much safer than what he did with the baby. He also stuffs himself with his own excrement because what is at home counts. At Easter, he put together a few samples. Kneads them and rolls them until they form an amorphous lump, which he edges and shapes with a knife until it forms a relatively apt lamb. He ties a red bow around its neck. He takes a picture of it and puts it on the desktop background. In the evening, he plays a concert that Enya played for the Pope and eats the whole lamb.

Something happened. Dominik needs change. No, not Dominik, but his stomach. The treasures found outside can no longer fully satisfy it. It asks for more, and Dominik suspects that he will have to satisfy it sooner or later. You just can't command your stomach. The stomach is not like a dog you tell sit or lie down and he will do it for you. The stomach isn't here to let itself rule, it won't take orders. Your stomach doesn't belong to you, you belong to your stomach. Dominik understands all this and definitely is not going to argue with it. No, he has to give it what *IT* wants. Dominik realizes that he is in a very difficult situation. Dominik is not crazy, even though most people probably wouldn't agree. He knows who he is. He belongs to the coprophiles. People taking pleasure in the smell of excrement. Some smear them all over their bodies. The vast majority of them are sexually aroused by excrement, but that's not Dominik's case. He never felt even the slightest sexual desire during collection, production, preparation, or consumption of the feces. Dominik never felt it because in addition to a certain affinity with coprophiles, he has completely unambiguous asexuality. Dominik isn't sexually excited by anything. He is convinced that this makes him a much more problematic individual in today's society than if he claimed to be a coprophile. Which he is not. He has just a slightly different diet. He doesn't bother anyone, he doesn't hurt anyone—except for that child in the pram, but it still won't remember anything. Dominik strongly doubts that his father will confide sometime in the future. And that old woman was JUST A LITTLE scared. Yeah, and then the two boys. It would be a problem if they shot it on their cell phones, but luckily, they didn't. So, apart from these cases, nothing happened.

But Dominik knows that something is different.

Dominik gets called in by the boss. Sasha is corpulent, almost two meters tall, silver-bearded, and has a bare skull. He orders Dominik to sit down and listen.

"The situation isn't going very well, you know."

Dominik nods. "Yes."

"I would see it this way. I'm offering you a seventy percent salary and you stay at home until I call you. "

"I understand."

"In these days, I need just one man in the office."

They stare at each other without a word for a few seconds.

"That's all," Sasha says.

"Should I go home?"

"Stay until the end of today. You're going to stay at home starting tomorrow."

Dominik gets up and is about to leave.

"Did you gain weight?" Sasha asks.

"Possibly." Although Dominik doesn't weigh himself, he never even bought a scale because it's useless for him, but he has fed a lot lately indeed.

"Just asking. You look better. Your cheeks are round, and you no longer look like you got out of a concentration camp."

"Thanks, boss."

Back in the office.

"What did he want from you?" Libor asks.

"I'm staying at home from tomorrow on."

"What?"

"He said that there is so little work that he needs only you."

"Well, thank you very much." Libor doesn't seem to be pleased. He hoped that he would be the one staying at home if it came to this. He has a lot of work around the house; he has to cut wood, the old wife wants to paint the kitchen white, he would also like to finally use the grill he bought last autumn with a fifty percent discount. Instead, he will rot in the office and risk a coronavirus infection.

"I'm not to blame," Dominik says.

"I know," Libor growls, returning to the Solitaire. He lifts himself a little in his chair and farts. Dominik feels it immediately. He actually felt it before it came. Libor is full of shit that can be dumped. He stares at the monitor and clicks to turn the cards over. Dominik approaches him and sucks in the air. Libor is even more grazed than Sasha and has been suffering from constipation lately. Dominik remembers how Libor bragged to him that when, after almost three days of constipation, he finally emptied himself, and then he stood on the scale and found himself to be four pounds lighter. Dominik shakes with excitement. When did Libor empty his guts the last time? Two or maybe three days? Then it's about time.

Dominik knows what he has to do. Change has come, and he needs to adapt.

"Do you want to go for a beer?" Dominik asks.

"And where, when everything is closed?"

"To my place. I have a few bottles in the fridge. "

Libor would like to have a beer, but his wife forbids it to him because he has to watch his weight and blood cholesterol level. Libor tries to drink in secret, just to drink a little, but that beast he married always recognizes it anyway.

"What about this evening?" Dominik suggests.

Libor scratches his head, thinking. "I'd have to call home."

An alarm starts shouting in Dominik. It's not a good idea.

"Why would you call?"

"If I don't call, she'll call," Libor says, pulling out his lower lip, which makes him look like an abnormally overweight child.

"Turn off your phone. Tell your wife the battery is drained."

"Dude, you don't know her. She's terribly cunning. What will I tell her when she asks me why I came so late?"

"You've been working overtime."

"She will smell beer on me."

"All right. Then you just tell her the truth. Your colleague is staying at home starting tomorrow, and whereas you won't see each other for a long time, you went to see him for a beer. "

Libor nods. "That's not bad."

"Definitely don't call her."

Libor shakes his head resolutely. "No, I won't."

"And turn off your phone."

Dominik leads Libor to a free car park. He explains that there will be no place in his street.

"Plus, they made blue zones there."

"Dickheads," Libor growled. "How far is it to you?"

"About two kilometres."

Libor moans. He is extremely tired already. By his sense of smell, Dominik knows that Libor's constipation is almost over. He will have to go to the toilet within a maximum of two hours, and this will happen at Dominik's place

Libor notices Dominik's gloves. "What are those for?"

"I don't want any prints left behind. Just kidding. I wear them when I'm outside.

You know, the infection."

"You're a jerk," Libor snorts, getting quickly out of the car.

At Dominik's.

"Can I take off this shit here?" Libor asks. By that shit, he means a face mask.

"Sure," Dominik says. "I'm not wearing it here either."

Libor sniffs. "Is there something wrong with waste pipes?"

"Yeah," Dominik said. "The plumber will come in a few days."

"He should as soon as possible, or you'll die from the stink."

"I'm almost used to it. I can light an incense stick if you want."

"That would be great."

Dominik plays a YouTube boxing match, Klitschko versus Joshua.

"I hope that moron gets his ass kicked," says Libor. "I'm don't watch this usually, I prefer hockey, but why not watch the two idiots beat the shit out of themselves sometimes . . . "

"Nicely said."

They pick up the bottles and tap. Dominik added a little laxative to Libor's bottle. After a while, Dominik disappears into the kitchen, where he has a painting drop cloth and several knives, which he had carefully sharpened last night. He spreads the drop cloth in the hallway and loads its edges with chairs.

"What are you doing there?" Libor shouted from the living room.

"Don't worry, nothing . . . "

Dominik returns to Libor. His colleague is ruddy in the face and starts sweating. His scent is almost unbearable. Dominik doesn't know what to do with his hands, he's still fidgeting, getting up, looking out the window, he's like a cat on hot bricks. He also can't sit well with that knife behind his belt. It was a good idea with the car, Dominik is an expert on good ideas, just keep it as far away from his address as possible.

"Did something bite you?"

"No," Dominik says.

"Then why are you pacing like a caged lion?"

Dominik sits down carefully and waits. It will happen soon. At the end of the match, Libor grunts and starts to get on his feet. He gives Dominik a guilty look and asks where his toilet is.

"I will show you."

He passes the radio, presses play, and Enya drives *Anywhere Is* to the fullest. Dominik places his hand on his colleague's shoulder and hides the other behind his back, where he grips the handle of the knife. "This way."

They leave the living room, and Libor asks why the fucking drop cloth is here and why he has to listen to the strange sectarian music for god's sake. It is the last question and the last sentence he says in his life.

The blade penetrates the fat neck. Libor raises his hands, looking surprised. The fingers of his right hand touch on the tip of the knife, it went through. A moment later, his knees break, and he goes to the ground. Dominik tries to hold him to soften the fall of the huge body. He pulls the knife out of Libor and stabs him between the shoulders. Puddles of blood form around Libor's head. Dominik knew this would happen, that's why the drop cloth. He pulls out the knife, laboriously turns Libor on his back, rolls up his T-shirt over his navel, unbuttons his pants, and pulls them down a little. Dominik must manage to do this while Libor is still alive. His colleague's eyes flutter frantically across the ceiling as if looking for traces of bad paint. Dominik runs to the kitchen and brings the rest of the knives. He probably won't use them all, but they are sharpened so nicely . . .

He stabs a short knife into the abdomen and makes a vertical incision to the pubic hair. More blood pours out of the wound. Dominik leads the second cut horizontally over the first. Then he opens Libor, revealing his colleague's digestive system in front of him. He tightly grips Libor's large intestine and pulls it out. It slips away the first time. So, he grips it even tighter, and when it's out, he reaches for the knife and cuts off the intestine from the rectum.

He checks on Libor; he's still alive but won't be for long. Now his time on Earth counts down to seconds.

Dominik lies on his back next to his colleague, puts the severed end of Libor's large intestine in his mouth, and starts pushing on it from top to bottom. His mouth is filled with hot and fresh excrement. There is so much food that he can't swallow all of it and has to take short breaks. Libor's head slips to the side, so the last thing he sees is Dominik, feeding on his shit. The brown matter flows down Dominik's cheeks and chin, it's in his hair, on his hands, mixes with the cooling blood. Libor stops breathing. Dominik swallows his food; it's a marvellous pile, but delicious, delicate, and spicy bitter. Dominik rolls it on his tongue, swallows, chokes again, and keeps squeezing the gut until it's empty.

It will take hours to clean up this mess, but Dominik doesn't mind it. It was beautiful, exceptional, quite possibly he experienced what Zen masters call nirvana.

He goes to the window, naked and still stained with food and blood. Twilight descends on the city, and the seemingly endless rows of lamps light up in the streets of the town. Under them, people will walk in their face masks, let out fragrant gases and attract Dominik . . .

And if not, Dominik will sniff them out. He is already extremely curious about what his stomach will come up with next.

LESHY

Lenny Ka

translated by Karolína Svěcená

DANA'S ANKLES WERE itching as the hard stalks of the grass rubbed against her skin. She stopped to scratch and uncertainly looked in the shadows under the branches of the pines standing on a gentle slope a few feet above her. Tom obviously didn't mind at all, or didn't have baby feet vulnerable to the sharp irritation of the grass, and he continued to walk directly to the trees at the edge of the coniferous forest.

"Bolet. It's as big as my leg," he shouted excitedly, pointing with his finger to places where she couldn't see from her position due to a stump surrounded by a protruding clump of grass.

"Don't yell so much," she warned him. Maybe they were not alone here. She felt someone's eyes on her for a while. Maybe it just seemed like that to her. Every now and then, she looked around to see if she could spot a pervert behind the trees and branches of low bushes. It could be a cyclist or another mushroom picker who had taken the same path as them. The forest lay just a short distance from one of the outskirts of Prague and, at this time, was usually full of people. But no matter how hard she looked, she didn't see anyone.

She only took a few steps to catch up with her brother. She fished a small knife out of her pocket and cut a mushroom just above ground overgrown with the dark green moss and grass. The ease with which the white mushroom yielded to the slicing blade indicated a fresh catch. She tentatively scratched a piece of the brown hat. Only pure yellowish tissue appeared under the blade, no traces of gnawing worms.

"Our first bolet." She smiled at Tom and placed the mushroom on the bottom of the wicker basket. She didn't miss the way his eyes lit up with joy. He didn't even wait for her, and without the slightest fear, he walked toward the pines. "Not this way." She stopped him. "We will continue through the glade. At its end is a narrow footpath leading down to the ravine." She indicated with her finger where to go, but he didn't look like he was going to listen.

"People will go there. We won't find anything there," he protested, but when he realized that she was ignoring his objections, he took a shuffling step behind her. With his head bowed, he probed the area for the brown heads of the mushrooms again. They could be around here in the glade in the low grass. Then he felt it. Instead of the warm touch of the sun's rays, a chill ran down his throat.

"Ggrrhhhch." There was a long, hoarse whine behind him.

"Dana!" he screamed and started running frantically.

Lenny Ka

The grass whipped at his ankles. On the sloping path, his legs were in danger of tangling in unyielding tufts. He could stumble and roll down the hill. But he didn't care. Terror cut into his bones. His sister walked just a few feet in front of him, and when she heard his screams, she turned and froze for a few seconds. He didn't understand that, he wouldn't stop for anything now. At the same time, her frightened expression forced him to speed up. He was looking for protection from her. What would he do if she didn't help him?

"Run!" She grabbed his sleeve as he caught up with her.

She pulled him behind her with such force that he stumbled several times. He was surprised he didn't fall and hit his knee. He couldn't run as fast as her. She was almost ten years older.

"We have to run down. We'll meet someone. Don't worry," she hissed between breaths. She needed most of the air she sucked into her lungs to keep running.

"Grrhhhhrrrggg." The thickets on the road just in front of them curled. Long black tracks flickered between the bushes as it tried to break through the leaves and unyielding branches. It was in front of them!

Dana yanked her brother aside. She veered out of the way and ran down the hillside, but the sleeves of his sweater inadvertently slipped from her palm. But she didn't stop. She zigzagged among the naked growing tree trunks. He ran after her, but her bright orange sweatshirt disappeared in the cluttered terrain in a few minutes. When he was alone, everything suddenly lost its meaning.

LESHY

Maybe he should hide somewhere. But where? There was a colorless gloom. The sun's rays did not penetrate here through the branches of aged conifers. With darker and darker shadows growing under the branches of the trees, a strange distress came upon him in unnatural silence. He wasn't running anymore. He couldn't catch his breath. He just crept quietly through the trees down the hill. Maybe his sister was waiting for him somewhere. She must have noticed that he was not running after her.

The loudness of his own breath terrified him. His heart was pounding so, he was afraid it would jump out of his body. When the pain gripped his throat, he didn't even scream, only his eyes swelled in their sockets as he fought for breath with the stranger's claws. In a futile desire to escape, he stretched his arms out in front of him. He tried to reach the branches of the nearest trees. Escape his prisoner. Kick him from behind to loosen the squeezing grip a little. But none of that happened. He could still feel the rough calluses of those thick fingers rubbing against his skin. Something hard and heavy clung to his sweaty shoulders. It breathed right in his face and smelled like rotting mud.

His throat burned so that tears welled up in his eyes. He wanted to scream in pain, but the compressed vocal cords made only a soft hiss. He desperately needed to breathe. He gasped for breath, but it didn't work. His lack of oxygen made his eyes twinkle. Saliva flowed from his open mouth and landed on rotting leaves and grass. He knew he was losing consciousness. So, he dug his child's fingernails into the strangling fingers and tried to kick again. But it was as if it were hitting the bark of a tree. The grip tightened. In the last flash of sanity, he heard an ominous thud. That's when black claws broke his neck.

* — ✦ — *

A thin trickle of blood flowed from the boy's nose. A small blood bubble formed just under his nose as the rest of the air came out of him. His skin was pale and soft. It just wanted to bite into it. The body attached to the boy's neck stopped fighting. Suddenly, it was as supple as a rag puppet. For a moment, the boy jerked a little in the death spasm.

It grabbed his hair and turned him so that his face was a short distance from it. Blood flowed from under his nose to his mouth and down to his chin. It licked it all in a second. But he wanted more. He needed more.

He opened the boy's mouth wide and pulled his tongue out. He bit into the soft pink tissue and jerked violently. He had so much blood in his mouth at once that he couldn't swallow it. He could feel the warmth and life pouring into his heart with it. Shit, he'd almost died.

She had saved him. Her intoxicatingly scented hair. Slender legs walking gracefully along forest paths. The rippling hips and breasts are just right enough to hold them in his palms. He had been watching her for several weeks. He always felt when she was in his woods, and he almost always had an erection.

However, the lymph returned to the body of clay, moss, and branches only slowly. He knew what he had to do. Throw her on the ground, thrust his erect dick into her, and fuck her until the whole universe danced with him. Only a connection with a man with warm blood circulating in his veins could bring him back to life.

But this was good too. He sucked the hot liquid flowing from the dying body and swallowed hungrily. It flowed into him, warming the cold entrails. But in a moment, the little one would be useless. The baby corpse cooled quickly in the dry evening. He looked into his face once more. His eyes were blue-gray, same as hers. They were still staring in terror. It seemed to him that in his unnaturally round pupils he saw, in addition to fear, a dumb accusation of the crime he had just committed. It was as if his stiff face with a bitten tongue and disfigured lips smeared with blood didn't look scary enough on its own.

But it had to be like this. He would never catch her, and if they both ran away, it would be hard for her to show up again soon. She was too scared to do that. But she will come for him. A woman always comes back for a child.

◆———◆———◆

Dana's knees broke with exhaustion. She sank into the grass and breathed heavily. It was as if someone was screaming terribly in the distance. But she heard nothing. There was a terrifying silence around her. The scream came straight from inside her. Tomas! Something bad must have happened to him. Should she go back for him? Maybe he was just a few meters behind her. She looked back. The slope of the hill she had just run up was empty. She saw only trees strewn with autumn yellow leaves.

"Tom?!?"

Lenny Ka

Nothing came back. Only the birds squealed in the distance. Several birds rose above the gorge below the treetops and flew confusedly in irregular circles. As she ran down the hill, she kept running fast. Up to the opposite slope. She had long since lost the basket with the mushroom. On the hill, just a few hundred meters from the forest, towered colorful blocks of flats in the Libuš housing estate. She would be safe there. She ran to the concrete towers with lighted windows. Somewhere halfway between the meadow behind the houses and the thinning trees, she stopped again.

Tom. Her little brother was still there. She took a few steps back and then stood, undecided. It would be best if she called her parents. But what would she tell them? After all, she left her brother alone in the forest. And she can't tell them that they were haunted by a bark and moss monster. They'd laugh at her. But she knew that what she saw on the other side of the ravine was not human. And the roar the creature made. Her eardrums had almost cracked.

"Tom?" She tried again. Only a gust of wind answered her. She should go for him. But she was terribly afraid to return. Plus, where to look for him? It had been about half an hour since she lost him. During that time, he could walk or run anywhere. She pulled a phone from her pocket and pressed the number on the screen.

"Hi, I'm over Modřanská ravine. Tom got lost. I have no idea what to do. "

Tom was found that evening by police handlers called by their parents. Mom sat on Tom's bed all night, squeezing his teddy bear and moaning softly. She just collapsed. In the morning, their father took her to a psychiatric hospital in Bohnice. But when the parents left and no one was crying in the apartment, it was even worse.

The silence was broken only by the regular ticking of the clock hanging on the wall. Evil could be hidden in every darkened corner. She saw his black claws reach for the blanket she was covered with. That's why she preferred to sleep in the light now. She slept for almost two days. They interrogated her before. First the police, then the psychologist. They showed her photos. She just told them that someone was chasing them through the woods. No, she doesn't remember what he looked like. When they saw that they would get nothing more from her, they gave her sedatives and sent her home.

<hr />

She was now sitting here on a rusty bench. Behind her back was a concrete housing estate from the 1980s. Prefabricated houses painted with bright colors, as if it can hide the moldy, smelly linoleum under the new paint. A dragonfly had just sat on a bush sprouting from the crack of the asphalt pavement. One quick move would be enough to crush it with her shoe. But she didn't want to stain her sole.

Strange. She had a rolled-up climbing rope in her backpack so she could say goodbye to this fucking world, but she didn't want to have a dirty shoe. She stared at the cracked asphalt. Holes of older date were more or less successfully punched by technical service staff. But new ones were created here. In the larger ones, grass sprouted, and its roots gradually changed the sidewalk into crumbling gravel. The ubiquitous shoots of lush vegetation, with their roots, leaves, and stems, relentlessly drilled through the reinforced concrete structure of the housing estate. Birds had built nests in the crevices, rust bit into the exposed iron, and rats and insect larvae enjoyed the cables. Nature took back in parts what people took from it. Lately, it seemed as if the degeneration of the outskirts of the city was progressing faster. The forest breathed and called her name.

She got up and headed there. She wouldn't go to the ravine. Definitely not. Just on the edge. On the rocks. She had a tree out there. It stood just above a steep rocky slope. Several of its branches grew so that they could reach them comfortably from the ground, but at the same time, they stuck into the space above the slope. She would tie a rope to one of them with a buckle, wrap the other end of the rope around her neck, and jump. She just had to be careful that no one saw her. But no one was in the meadow leading to the cliff. Why would they, the sun had not shone at all today. Heavy gray clouds soaked in the rain covered the sky. The wind picked up, suggesting that the downpour was not far away.

＊━━━◈━━━＊

Fuck. Another drop of water fell on his back. Why did it have to start wanting right now? He lay huddled under the trunk of a young uprooted pine tree too thin to protect him from the rain. He took a deep breath. With oxygen soaked in moisture and the scent of pine bark, he breathed something else into his lungs. The smell of dark hair, soft brown skin, and the provocative scent of a young woman's lap. Was it her, or did it just seem so to him? He waited in vain for her for three whole days. She tricked him, that little bitch. When the guys with the dogs appeared in the woods, it was clear to him that they were looking for him. Of course, they were mainly after the little boy. When they found him, they let the dogs go, and they ran across the forest like mad. They combed it for several hours.

Lucky he could blend in perfectly with the trees. He'd climbed on one of the spruces, hugged it around the trunk, and closed his eyes. He heard them and felt them walking around. The dogs felt him too. They dug their claws into the bark and barked furiously. They tried to crawl up behind him. When he felt the light of a flashlight on his skin, he almost felt scared. But the cops didn't see him. They pulled their beasts to their feet and went to snoop elsewhere. But he shivered and pressed against the bark long after they left.

He was not strong enough yet. But that would soon change, and then he would show them. He felt heat build up in his crotch. The lymph in his intestines flowed faster. The bark began to peel from his body, and green-gray skin appeared beneath it. So far, it was too sensitive to touch, but a newfound force was already working beneath it. It woke everything around. The city and its the people took energy from the forest for so long that he fell into a kind of vegetative state. He saw almost nothing and did not defend himself as they sawed and tore the roots off the ground so they could build more monstrous reinforced concrete boxes in their place.

"Grrhhhuuu." A howling roar came from inside him. That was it. He stood on all fours and jumped. Despite his massive physical construction and lingering stiffness, he was able to move surprisingly fast. He headed for the edge of the forest. To the rocks. Where he suspected her.

+ — • — + — • — +

She reached out her hand and touched one of the young shoots of the branch. She slowly pulled it closer to reach the mother branch from which it grew. She squinted against the cloudy sky to protect her eyes from the cold raindrops that pounded on her cheeks. A bit more. She got on her tiptoes and finally caught the smooth bark of a strong branch. Now to wrap the climbing rope around it. She reached for her belt, which she had previously grasped a metal clasp to hold, and carefully unbuckled the clasp. She pushed the branch as close to her as possible and began to wrap the rope around it. It went pretty bad because wet leaves and tiny twigs prevented her from doing so, but in the end, she succeeded. She fastened the buckle and slowly released the branch so that the rope would not slip out of her hand. She still has to tie a knot, put a noose around her neck, and jump. She stared at the sharp edges of the protruding stones below her. There was a narrow path between them, which could be reached down when one knew where to go.

Once, she could get down in pumps with a bottle of wine in her purse and glasses in hand. Those were the times. She was sixteen then. Martin and Šárka were waiting for her under the ravine by the lake. And her biggest problem back then was how to take the bottle with the glasses unnoticed from home and not kill herself on the way down the rock.

She blinked to get tears from her eyes. She still had to tie the knot.

He paused for a moment to look around. The forest in front of him thinned. Behind the crossroads lay a small glade. There were a couple of wooden chairs and tables for people from the city to have picnics by the lake. A rocky slope rose behind him. His heart almost stopped when he saw her on a rock in front of him tying a rope to a branch. Now he couldn't scare her. He had to get as close to her as possible unnoticed, so he wouldn't go straight across the clearing. He would rather go around the open space, where she could easily see him, by detour hidden under the trees. He jumped. Upon impact, he sank lightly into the rain-damp clay. The mud slowed him down. He couldn't bounce so well on it. What the hell was she doing up there? He narrowed his eyes to get a better look through the obscuring branch.

Dana held a tied noose in her hands. All she had to do was put it over her head and run down the stone. Almost as if she had slipped. *Does dying hurt, or is it like falling asleep?* Maybe then she'd see Tom again. How he laughed and played. She knew he would die if she ran away and left him in the woods. And instead of helping him, she'd let go of his hand and left him at the mercy of the monster. She deserved to die. She pulled the noose over her head and closed her eyes. Just swing down. To the abyss.

No. He bounced off the ground and landed on a rock. *She must not kill herself!* He estimated that she was about twenty, at most thirty meters away. He had to now use all his strength to be with her before she jumped off the rock. He bounced sharply until small pieces of rubble flew off his feet. During the landing, he caught a nearby trunk of a pine tree. He took a breath and jumped again. The falling rocks caught her attention. She opened her eyes and stared straight at him, frightened. The distance between them was halved.

✦ ━━✦━━ ✦

Dana could almost physically feel the blood clot in her veins. He was just below her. From the body overgrown with dark green moss and the shoots of the branches with the inconsistently sprouting leaves, four flexible claws grew, from which the monster bounced like an overgrown toad. The moss detached on several parts of his torso and hung from it in lines from which a greenish liquid dripped. Bark and soaking gray tissue shone through the moss. His red eyes mesmerized her with a lustful look, and a blackened tongue flickered between his puffy lips.

The beast jumped again. It was so close that she could smell the muddy stench of its body.

She slipped her feet down from the stone. The sharp impact of the tightening loop caused by the gravity of her body took her breath away. She didn't have a millimetre left to suck air into her empty lungs. The rough rope cut into the skin on her neck. She grabbed it instinctively with both hands in a futile attempt to loosen it and breathe a little. Her legs tried to find any support in the open space, but the noose tightened around her neck tighter. The weight of her own body crushed her spine. Broken nerves sent terribly painful spasms into the dying body. She no longer noticed that he was almost by her.

By the time he finally lifted her limp body and roughly pushed it up onto the stone, she was already dead.

He tore her water-soaked clothes to reach her hot skin and blood-throbbing body. He hugged her to warm her and held his breath. He hoped he could feel a faint heartbeat beneath her skin. She was still warm, but the blood in her veins was no longer flowing. Her blue-gray eyes were open wide and blank as death had taken her. When he pulled off her pants and slid her panties to the side, he could shove his dick into her soft fragrant pussy and save her.

He wanted to fuck her from the moment he saw her. Touch her delicate skin. Kiss her. Lick pink nipples. Feel her from the inside. His cock hardened even now as he touched her and looked at her breasts. He needed to do it. Squirt out all the accumulated sperm. And with it, pass on part of his self to her. A piece of his own life, which she had previously given him. Then she would open her eyes and look at him with that mischievous and a little grateful look. She would stroke him all over and also in the crotch. Caress his dick and shove it in her mouth.

But somehow, he couldn't. His chest burned and his throat tightened so he couldn't even shout. He just watched the remnants of energy slowly fade from her body. But if he didn't do something, her soul would leave the shadows and never find its way back again among the living. Her cheeks would fall and her skull bones emerge. Then she wouldn't be pretty at all. He bent down and kissed her on the lips. He licked them a little. Then he put his finger to the dimple between her breasts with nipples swollen from cold. He pushed it down slowly, pressing a little with the sharp tip of his claw.

A small groove appeared above the ribs, filling with blood. He licked it. What if he bit her a little . . . not much, otherwise he would hurt her and she would never wake up. He squeezed one of her nipples between his teeth and bit. The metallic rawness of the blood completely stunned him. It was as if a truck had hit his brain. He bit deeper and deeper. When there was nowhere to continue, he bit her other breast. His whole face and hands were covered in blood. The red human lymph poured strength into his body and calmed him a little. He moistened his erect dick with her blood. He ripped her panties off and shoved it into her.

At first, he had trouble getting deeper into her, she was too narrow and tight, but then it went much better. He closed his eyes. He found her lips with his tongue and bit into them. The smell, the taste of blood, and the intense friction against her vagina excited him so much that he ejaculated in a moment. When he pulled away from her, instead of beautifully rounded breasts with red nipples, only the remnants of bleeding flesh were on her chest. A dark blue bruise began to flow under her bitten lip.

He shook her. Nothing. Her eyes were as dead as before. He lifted her a little and shook her hard again. She didn't wake up. Instead, her head fell to the side and a long trickle of soppy blood came out of her mouth. He crawled into the air for a moment like a small snake trying to reach from a height to solid ground. But then gravity prevailed and the blood began to fall in small drops onto the gray surface of the stone and splash on it.

A deep roar escaped his throat, making his blood run cold. It was his fault. He hurt her. He began rubbing her chest with his palms to bring her life back to her, along with the warmth, but she didn't even tremble. He didn't stop. He kept trying until his arms burned in pain. But it was useless. How could he? Blurred blood mingled with his tears. He couldn't save her. His head rumbled unbearably. He looked at the rope on which she hung herself and then at the cloudy sky.

He felt much stronger now, yes, but he was also completely empty. He had to find another one. One day, one would definitely come. She would be alive and well and only his. Forever.

VLTAVA CLAY

Edward Lee

"**AW, COME ON, JAKE!**" Susan complained. Then she thought, *Ug! Fuck! "There* again?"

Jake chuckled like he always did. "You know you love it, baby. Besides, we're celebrating our new place to live!"

MY new place to live, Susan corrected him.

He bent her over harder on the table, grabbed her hips, then hooted, "Choo choo! All aboard the buttfuck express!"

Yeah, this is some prize of a boyfriend I have, huh? Susan only had time to grit her teeth and close her eyes before—

"Yup! That's the ticket!" Jake announced.

—the hot, spit-lubed erection slammed into her sphincter and started going to town. Susan's face felt stiff as a wooden mask. Every time his dick popped into her, it was like taking a shit in reverse, and sometimes she wondered if it was worth it. This was the price she had to pay for his company? Getting reamed?

The table legs shuddered. Before long came the

arrival of his inane, bestial grunts; she frowned at the sensation of the hot spurts invading her bowel. *Yuck,* was all she could think. *Why do I put up with this?*

She knew the answer, of course: she hated being alone, and having recently turned forty, suitors weren't exactly standing in line. Not with her tits sagging, her belly bulging, and bags growing beneath her eyes. Such was the tenor of Susan's desperate insecurities. *I let this redneck hooligan put his cum up my ass every day because I can't stand the thought of him leaving.* She was even pretty sure he was cheating on her, yet she didn't dare mention it.

"Aw, fuck, baby . . . that was great. You're a peach!"

Yeah, a peach with a sore butt. She could've imagined the sound of a cork popping when he pulled out of her. She just lay bent over the table with her belly pressed down, trying to re-collect herself. *So this is really what it's all about?*

He patted her ass as afterplay. "I'm gonna go take a shower"—he chuckled—"gotta wash your shit off my dick!"

"Charming," she muttered.

When he was off, she put her pants back on and was stricken by an instant grimace from the feel of the poop-smear in her butt-crack. *Damn him,* she thought. *Fucker. What is it with men, anyway? They always gotta put it in the wrong hole.* This was not the best impression with which to start the first day in her new abode. She tried to remind herself that she should be happy. She looked around the cramped, cluttered apartment stacked with moving boxes and still couldn't believe it was hers now, by the provisions of her late Uncle Petr's will. At least it was paid for, and all she had to shell out herself were the utilities and a small condo fee, so this would definitely help her and Jake's financial situation. But– *Looks smaller than last time I was here.* When had that been? Last Christmas? Yet even with the clutter and seeming smaller, the place felt hollow without the wizened, balding form of Uncle Petr stumbling around and talking of the great times in the Old Town of Prague, the *Stare Maestro*, spinning his tales in his high piping voice and clipped Czech accent. But she had to wonder how "great" those times had really been since he'd been born shortly after World War II, when Prague was a ruin and Czechoslovakia had been an impoverished Soviet satellite. Somehow, he'd emigrated here in the '70s.

The back wall of the tiny living room boasted a score of photos of Prague: the majestically spired Prague Castle on the hilltop over the winding river; the gothic Charles Bridge, which had protected the city from invaders since the 1300s; the entry to the Old Jewish Cemetery, the home of 100,000 graves, the oldest of which was dug in 1432; and, of course, a spacious shot of the Old Town Square, the heart of the city since the 11th Century. Most of these were older framed photographs, most in black and white and no doubt taken by Uncle Petr himself when a teenager. As fascinating as these old places were, Susan found them tinged by the brooding pall of the communist era. Such observations, certainly, would inspire reflection in most modern-day Americans: what was it like to have one's childhood in Post World War II Czechoslovakia and to grow up in Communist

Prague? *Uncle Petr must've had a hard as shit life before he escaped to the US,* Susan considered, but her contemplations didn't delve much deeper than that. No, Susan was a typical Facebook and Starbucks American, not particularly interested in the world that churned around her unless it involved a new "app" or a new social media outlet. She did have a college degree in Art History, though, and she could talk all day about Abstract Expressionism and the Dada Movement and Max Ernst and Thomas Hart Benton—but regrettably, such a sheepskin only got her a job as assistant manager of Captain Salty's Seafood Shack. At least her standard American obliviousness kept her deaf, dumb, and blind to the more introspective notions in life. She even knew she had much to be grateful for: her job was adequate and provided her a living, her all-but-useless boyfriend kept loneliness at bay, and now this little condo left to her by her uncle would ease her finances.

And that reminded her . . .

She and her uncle had shared a common enthusiasm in the past: they were both ceramic artists . . . or *had been,* in her case. In college, Susan had taken several pottery classes to accommodate her degree, while Uncle Petr had gladly encouraged her in that direction, for he'd made a living as a ceramic artist for decades and was quite skilled. When younger, Susan had even gone with him to various arts and crafts shows about the state to help him sell his wares: typical items such as vases; hand-painted pumpkins, fruits, frogs, toad, salamanders, and the like; and elves, sprites, and trolls. It didn't sound like much, but the painstaking attention to detail, plus his personal little flourishes, seemed to make Uncle Petr's merchandise more attractive to the customers, and he always took home impressive sums.

Maybe I'll get back into it, she mused, unconvinced. Pottery *was* a creative outlet, and perhaps that's what she needed to get her out of her mid-life doldrums. She meandered down the hall past the bedroom, then into the den, which served for Uncle Petr's workroom. Here was the old kick-spin potter's wheel that had seen half a century of use, and here, the newer electric kiln, which she guessed would bring at least $500 on eBay. A potter's room was always a mess and always filled with the redolence of old clay, but this earthy, semi-cloying scent was something she liked, for it reminded her of other, happier times when she'd been more involved with herself.

Beneath the work table sat the large lidded crate that contained Uncle Petr's clay—mostly of the iron-free kaolin variety, which emitted a slightly earthy but clean and nearly spicy scent. Next to this, though, sat a much larger crate, and something not quite conscious compelled her to open it. *Oh, wow!* she thought, for the clay in *this* crate possessed a stronger redolence, almost musky, which she found vaguely arousing. What filled most of it was not square parcels of commercially packed clay—like in the first crate— but basketball-sized portions of clay roughly wrapped in heavy-gauge clear plastic. The clay itself appeared dark gray mixed with dark green. There must've been at least six such portions. It seemed sad, reflecting upon this logistic: Uncle Petr had all this clay for an abundance of future pottery projects . . . but now, those projects would never be realized.

The observation cheapened her mood; she knew she'd be lying to herself to think that she would resume her old interests in ceramic art; she was too unmotivated. *And I'm too unmotivated to sell all this stuff, which means I'll have to throw it out.* It would almost be like throwing Uncle Petr himself out . . .

Damn it! And at once, she was nearly in tears. She pushed herself out of the room and fled to the second-story balcony. The moon lurked behind the trees beyond the parking lot; the mild spring night seemed like a freeze-frame. What seemed to lurk along with the moon was her depression. It had always been there, she knew, but it was Uncle Petr's death that amped it up. Her uncle had been a lonely old man for a long time, and he'd died alone. Now came the rain of regrets . . .

I should've visited him more often, I should've called more. Fuck. Always putting it off, always too busy. She lit a cigarette and spewed smoke in self-disgust. She tried to let her thoughts neutralize, let the shitty mood rise away with the cigarette smoke.

The murmur of television could be heard next door, then she heard two people come out to the balcony beside her. Two snaps of cigarette lighters were heard.

"How was work?" asked a woman.

"The usual. It sucked," answered a man. "The new hosebag secretary needs to be cunt-punted into the next zip code, and the new account manager must have her pussy where her brain should be and someone just gangbanged it."

"You're so profane!" The woman laughed, but then her tone tuned hostile. "And that motherfuckin' boss of yours . . . *You* should've been given that manager position; you have fuckin' seniority."

"Yeah, but I don't suck dick like Little Oral Annie, so that's that. Welcome to reality."

"That cheap tight-wad motherfucker—"

Susan was astounded by the heights of the couple's cursing, especially the woman's, who then added: "I'll bet he's a fuckin' Jew."

The man laughed. "Honey, his last name is Katzenburger. Ya think?"

"Well, at least the old Jew next door is finally in the ground. The fucker must've been a hundred. Best thing is we won't have to smell that Gefilte fish shit anymore."

"And whatever that onion crap was, that'd stink up the whole building." The man paused. "Speaking of kikes, has anyone moved into his place yet? I think I just saw lights on inside tonight."

"Oh, yeah, the landlord told me his daughter or niece or some shit inherited the place, and I heard people over there today."

"Great," sniped the man. "One Jew bites the dust, and another takes his place . . . "

Wincing, Susan put out the cigarette and went back inside. She'd honestly never heard so much anti-Semitism at once in her life. *Is that a thing now?* And how anyone could harbor ill-will toward her uncle was baffling; he was a simply a nice old man who hadn't an unkind word against anyone.

People are just shitty all over, I guess, she concluded. *They need scapegoats to blame for their problems rather than own up to their own inadequacies.* Though non-practicing, she was Jewish herself and didn't see that she was different from anyone else in any way.

The overheard conversion only soiled more of her mood. When she peeked down the hall, she saw Jake walking nude from the bathroom to the bedroom, which reminded her that he had to work tonight. Shitty boyfriend or not, she didn't want to be alone the first night in her new home.

"Why didn't you tell me you were working tonight?" she wanted to yell but asked calmly.

"Sorry, babe." He was a security guard at a warehouse somewhere. "Thought I did."

"Damn it. I wanted us to be together for our first night here."

He pulled his navy-blue pants up over the bigger-than-average-sized penis, and then he winked at her. "Can't stand to be without me, huh?"

"Fuck!" she replied and stormed to the kitchen. She poured a glass of wine, grumbling, then sat dejected in Uncle Petr's armchair. Was she *that* insecure? *That* uncomfortable alone with her own thoughts? *I guess I'm just vapid,* she thought.

Now Jake was buttoning up his security tunic as he walked out to the living room. "Got another double shift tonight, hon—"

Susan's shoulders slumped even more.

"—so's I probably won't see you 'til tomorrow afternoon . . ."

Here was more of her insecurity, which infuriated her. This wasn't the first time she'd heard the "double-shift" spiel, and she sure didn't see much evidence of it in his paychecks. *I know damn well he's cheating on me. THAT'S his double shift. So why don't I confront him about it, or put one of those direction thingies on his car?*

The answer was simple. She didn't want to know.

If I caught him, then he'd leave.

Jake chuckled as he put on his leather gun belt. "You know, babe? We got time for a quickie if you want."

You just came up my ass, you asshole! she wanted to scream. "I'm not a love doll, you know," she sputtered.

"Well, you're sure as hell *my* beautiful doll, and I sure as hell love you," he said. This was the best she was going to get from him as far as endearments went.

Fuck. I'm such a wuss . . . "Okay, come here," she said, and he walked right up to her, his crotch exactly face-level with her. At least he'd taken a shower after having it in her ass. Smirking, she unhooked the belt and let it thunk to the floor, then fumbled open his trousers. By now, it was all auto-pilot, and she supposed that it was ingrained in her. It was the Rule of a Woman's Life: *If you want to keep a man, you suck his dick, like, ALL THE TIME.* So she sucked and sucked and sucked. It didn't take him long, so she guessed that meant her technique was formidable. When the first spurt started, she yanked his butt cheeks open to give his prostate a jig, and then—

Here it comes . . .

"Ah, fuck, honey," he groaned, clamping her head so he could fuck it.

One loop after another filled up her mouth; she didn't bother counting them anymore because that just seemed to make the process last longer.

"Ah, that's my baby," he muttered. He pulled his dick out of her mouth, where it dangled, letting a single squiggle of sperm flip off the end, to and fro. "Yes, sir, I got me the best fuckin' girlfriend in the world . . ."

Wincing, she looked for a place to spit, found none, so just swallowed with a typical grimace.

"Love you, babe," he said, re-buckling his belt, and then he kissed her on the top of her head. "Gotta run. See ya tomorrow."

"Yeah," she croaked.

He couldn't have left the condo any faster.

The instant the door closed, she felt worse; she felt hollowed out. The room seemed to darken faster than the sinking sun. *Don't sit around and mope!* she implored herself. *Snap out of it!* If this kept up, she'd have to see a counselor, get on meds. It was ridiculous to feel this melancholy all the time when she really had nothing to feel bad about. It took all her effort to heave herself from the chair, disrobe, and take a shower.

First, she opened her mouth to the spray, trying to wash out that awful sperm aftertaste, but it had never worked in the past and didn't work now. But when she closed her eyes and sudsed herself up, she started to feel better. She imagined the suds were her disconsolation and the brisk spray was washing it all down the drain, taking it far away from her. Next, her hand worked the bar of soap intricately between her legs. When her finger slipped up the tender groove, she actually felt a sharp, pleasant spark, something that hadn't happened for a while. *Give it a shot,* she thought and then began to imagine her own hands had become the hands of some big, muscular man standing behind her, and those hands were sliding all over her body as if molding her. Big deliberate fingers tweezed her nipple-ends, then corkscrewed them with just the right amount of torque so that she nearly yelped from the pain. She also imagined a sizable, hard cock sticking up like a prong between her back and his belly; then she tried to carry the fantasy farther, where she'd be very unceremoniously bent over and invaded from behind, not in her ass this time but right up her pussy. *Holy shit, I've got to come!* she thought, and it was a very desperate thought. Her knees were wobbling in the shower; her hand snatched her sex and tried to work its way into her, to the wrist, but she couldn't quite make that work. Susan rarely got this horny, the doldrums of life having chased most of her real desires away, yet here she was now . . .

Fuck! I've got to do something about this!

She bolted out of the shower and out of the bathroom, not even drying off. She giggled to herself, imagining how she must look: a sopping-wet middle-aged frump running around nude in a sexual frenzy. No, simple masturbation wouldn't do, not for this. *I need to STICK something in me, bad! Right now!* In the cramped living room, she was nearly stumbling over the stacked moving boxes. There weren't that many, so it shouldn't take long to find the one that contained her vibrator. On her knees, she plowed into the boxes, tore each one open and rummaged almost maniacally, but—

Fuck! Fuck-fuck-fuck!

The vibrator wasn't to be found.

She whined aloud, then jumped up and thudded to the kitchen. She popped open cabinets, dragged open drawers. From one drawer, her hand snatched up a long plastic salad spoon, which she stared at cock-eyed, winced, then tossed it away. *I can't stick that in myself, for shit's sake!* Next, she pulled up a turkey baster. *Maybe this would work . . . I could stick it in backwards . . .* But, no, with her luck, the squeeze bulb would come off and she'd probably have to go to the hospital to have it removed. She flung the thing away.

There were no wine bottles, and the only beers her uncle drank were in cans. The liverwurst in the fridge was too big, and the zucchini was wilted.

DAMN it! She shouted the thought and slammed the fridge door.

Candles? No, too thin. A can of Pam butter-flavor cooking spray? No, too thick. The thinner can of Jake's shaving gel might suffice for width, but how would she get it into herself? She rushed to the laundry room but . . .

Am I really gonna stick a mop handle in my pussy? Am I THAT desperate and fucked up in the head?

She didn't wait for an answer to the question. But next she found herself in Uncle Petr's workroom, and . . .

Wait a minute. The pottery clay . . .

She was on her knees in a flash and looking back in the crates of various sorts of modeling clay. A lot of it was fireable clay, and she wasn't confident using the kiln after so many years. *Naked Woman Burns Down Apartment Making Dildo,* she could see the headline. One crate, however, contained plasticine clay, the hand moldable type but—

Fuck, she thought. It all was too old and had mostly hardened. This left the last, larger crate. She hadn't noticed it before, but the word VLTAVA was written on the lid in magic marker, Uncle Petr's scrawl, no doubt, and also 30 DUBEN 68, but the little bit of Czech she'd learned from her parents and Uncle Petr had long since dissipated with time.

The old lid's hinges creaked when she slowly lifted it, and she half-noticed that her excitement had risen a notch, hormones firing away in her brain. Was it the scent of the clay? This uncharacteristic horniness was making her antsy; she could feel a pulse beating in her sex. Yes, that earthy, heady scent drifted back to her nostrils; she could feel her heart-rate jump up. When she leaned over, her breasts swayed, brushing her nipples across the crate's edge; the sensation caused her to wince from a luscious discomfort that made her slap her hand to her pubis and squeeze. *What the fuck is wrong with me? I'm NEVER this horny . . .* Of course, the reason was easy to assume: more than a month since her last orgasm on top of the fantasy in the shower, and her brain chemistry was having a heyday.

So now I'm scrambling to make a dildo with my dead uncle's clay!

This darker clay in the last crate was well-sealed in the plastic bags; though firm, it hadn't hardened. But she was up again, fumbling through her uncle's tools, looking for something she could use to excise a sufficient chunk.

From amongst a splay of potter's tools, she grabbed a metal chisel with a wide blade, then leaned into it, eventually cutting out a wedge about a foot long. Penetrating the surface of the primary mass of clay caused the material to release even more of that alluring, earthy aroma. Her nostrils flared; she sighed and touched her sex again. What was it about that scent? Something vaguely musky intermingled with something vaguely sweet and not unlike honeysuckle. Whatever it was, it was stoking her sexual awareness in ways she'd never experienced. It made her feel slightly high, it made her salivate, it made her nipples stick out and ache. Next, without being conscious of it, she hustled to her uncle's work table and—*THUD THUD THUD!*—was pounding the wedge of clay with a wooden mallet and, in a few minutes' time, had wrought out a nice, well-rounded column, just over two inches thick, just over a foot long. The object's lack of total uniformity gave it an enticing sort of "organic" look. The more she held it in her hands, the more distance she felt from her volition. Yes, she was horny as hell, wincingly so. Was the dildo actually throbbing in her hands? No, of course not, but she probably imagined it as her pulse beat.

Fuck this, she thought; she didn't even take the time to trot to her bed. Instead, she sat bare-assed right down on the floor, lay back, and thrust her legs apart. Impulse brought the dildo's rounded end to her mouth to slick it up with spit. It tasted like absolutely nothing, but its wetness only sharpened that beguiling scent. Her hands visibly shook as she brought the column of clay to bear.

What are you waiting for? she thought. *Stick the damn thing in your cooter!*

And so she did. It sank into her so easily it almost felt *sucked* in; she tensed up, groaned, and shivered.

Hooooly SHIT, that feels good . . . Her mind swam, and with each slow penetration of the dildo into her flesh, and with each slow withdrawal, her body felt as though it were being stretched out by force. She tried to resummon her fantasy lover from the shower, but he wouldn't come. Then she tried several other ploys: imagining past lovers or movie stars, but . . . *Damn it* . . . each image only distracted her and eventually dissolved. All the while her hand continued easing the clay dildo into and out of herself, each stroke kindling more sensations, yet with her mind not fixing on an appropriate image, her pleasure kept distancing itself.

Come ON!

She decided she must be trying too hard. So, she let her mind sink into darkness, and, sure enough, a different image appeared out of no conscious conjuring of her own. A man? No . . . a phantom, perhaps the entity she'd imagined in the shower. *Faceless, voiceless, but big and strong, all muscle and cock. The perfect man* . . . She closed her eyes, and that did the trick. Her horniness—hormones, brain chemistry, whatever—lit right up when she imagined herself being mauled on the floor by this faceless, intent *thing.* Hot hands more like mittens groped her, pressed her body down into the floor, cupped her breasts and squeezed. Susan's legs splayed lewd and wide, her hips jutting upward. Her lover's form almost seemed boneless, the fingerless mitts for hands shaping themselves around her own physique, imbuing her with more heat and desire as she squirmed beneath them. Her body was being used as a plaything, a curio of flesh, by this manifestation of her own mind, and as all those dense, sexual sensations hammered down into her nerves, the less aware she was of her own hands plunging the dildo in and out and the more aware she was of the idea that her consciousness was seeping out of her eyes, floating upward, and looking down like someone's near death experience. She was watching herself, yes, watching herself writhe in groaning, drooling, guttural ecstasy while her body was being rutted. Susan could see herself lying with painfully spread legs as her hands manipulated that elongation of brownish, grayish clay in and out of her sex, her vagina, her squirming pussy, each venture deeper titillating more raw nerves. However, over her body, something else lurked, a barely delineated outline like a superimposition. It was a figure, all right, some hulking, mindless *thing* humping her, drilling into her, trying to get more and more of its otherworldly cock stuffed ever deeper into her flesh. Now the apparition began to hump harder, and she could see the vague outline of its bulk shift; its mitt-hands groping her, and one of them girded her throat and squeezed. She screamed silently to herself, her body beginning to convulse as terror seized her, and then her floating consciousness was yanked back into her body as her heart began to skip beats and that inhuman hand collared her throat even harder. The barely-visible beast's other hand covered her mouth and nose as the chokehold heightened. Susan's terror had nowhere to go now, yet her hands still desperately pistoned the dildo. Her orgasm broke at the same moment she thought she would surely suffocate, and her entire body clenched in and out in a death seizure with an explosion of endorphins that flooded her brain, leaving her to flop on the floor like a hauled-in fish. The sensation felt so good that she didn't even care that she might be dying for real.

Holy shit . . .

In the lull that followed, the only sound to be heard was a clock ticking somewhere. She couldn't move and didn't want to, choosing instead to lie there nude on the workroom's floor, sated, half-smiling, eyes closed. Was she actually drooling? *Best orgasm of my life,* came a murmuring thought. *Fuck, I need to indulge myself more often. God knows I've earned it . . .* This much was true. Her next inclination was to get up and get back to unpacking, but at that precise moment, the prospect seemed impossible. She was just too tired. Her climax had pilfered the last of her energy. The image she had of herself just then was so comical, she chuckled. Naked, sprawled on the floor, a make-shift dildo at her groin? It had slipped out of her by now, of course, and made a tiny *thunk,* but she didn't even have the energy to wash it off and put it away. She chuckled again.

A moment later, she was sound asleep.

<hr/>

She awoke in clot-like darkness that seemed tinted with throbs of red and blue light. When she leaned up off the floor, she had to re-collect herself. Yes, she'd fallen asleep there after masturbating herself into an explosive climax. There were no sounds, just the same mantle clock ticking; it was 4 a.m. And what were those throbbing lights? She dragged herself to her feet amid a slight chill—*Of course! I got no clothes on!* But before going for her robe, she felt that she must investigate the throbbing lights; had she not been so drowsy, she would've recognized them at once.

Flashing red and blue lights?

Oh, fuck . . .

They were coming from outside through the workroom window. *Must be from the parking lot.* She pulled her blouse back on, moved out to the living room, and edged toward the sliding door. She'd obviously forgotten to close the door earlier, for it stood open a few inches. This explained the chill. But she didn't step completely out onto the balcony, not so skimpily dressed. Instead, she stood on her tiptoes and visually verified what, by now, she already knew.

Damn! What happened?

The parking lot down below was filled with emergency vehicles, mostly police cars but also several ambulances and—Susan gulped—a white step van that read METRO MEDICAL EXAMINER.

Had a resident died? Uncle Petr had only been one of many elderly residents in this condo complex. *But why so many cop cars? For a heart attack or stroke, something like that?* The observation left a strange impression, and so did the creepy red and blue lights tinting the darkness inside the condo. She rushed to flick some lights on, then found her robe just in time to jump from the start of someone knocking rather loudly on her front door.

She rushed to the door, then froze. *It's four in the morning; you don't just open your door when someone knocks . . .* In the peephole stood a very tall man in a dark suit and tie, however warped, and she did make out the image of a badge on a breast pocket.

"Uh, can I help you?" she called through the door.

A toneless male voice replied, "This is Deputy Chief Spence of the Metro Police Department's Major

Case Squad. I'd like to talk to you about your neighbors. If you're uncomfortable opening your door at this hour, may I give you my phone number and we can talk that way?"

Susan paused. The fact that he'd given her the option allayed any fears she might have. Instead, she opened the door.

Suddenly, she faced a tall, big block of a man, well over six feet, with short gray hair, broad shoulders like a weightlifter's, in a tailored suit just darker than charcoal-gray. Estimating his age was well-nigh impossible.

"Please pardon the imposition," he said, "but—"

"Is everything all right?" she asked out of impulse. "All those emergency vehicles outside—"

"Yes, well, how well did you know the Wittmans?"

She stared. "I, um, I don't. Who are they?"

Spence gestured to her left. "Your next door neighbors."

Susan noticed uniformed police coming and going and heard a racket of other doors being knocked on. "I'm sorry. Please come in."

He nodded and moved through the door.

Damn, this guy is big, she thought. *What was he saying?* "And I'm afraid I don't know the neighbors at all. In fact, I just moved here today."

The man stilled at this information, then squinted at a card. "And where is . . . Petr . . . Knispel?"

"He's deceased, I'm sorry to say," Susan said. "I'm his niece, Susan Knispel. Uncle Petr left me this condo in his will."

Spence's eyes slowly roved back and forth as he talked. "I'm sorry for your loss, Ms. Knispel. The reason I'm here is . . . well, your neighbors, the Wittmans, I'm afraid, were killed sometime, we think, over the last four hours."

Susan's mouth fell open as a breath caught in her chest. "My God . . . The couple next door? I never met them, but I did hear them talking when I was smoking on my balcony earlier—"

Spence withdrew a notepad. "And what time was that?"

She pressed her memory. *It was right before I sucked Jake's dick, wasn't it?* "Um, five, five-thirty, I think. Shortly before my boyfriend Jake left for work."

"Ah, boyfriend. His name, please?"

"Jake Radley. He's a security guard at the Villar's warehouse, which is nearby . . . " and then she gave him Jake's number. "But I doubt that he could've had any contact with the neighbors."

Spence nodded, scribbling. "And back to them, the neighbors. You said you heard them talking on their balcony. Do you recall what they said? Anything that you might regard as unusual?"

The question blanked in her mind. "You said . . . the Wittman's were killed? Do you mean . . . *murdered?*"

Spence kept shooting glances about the living room, as if in some vague assessment. "We don't know yet; they still need to be examined by the medical examiner's office."

"Oh. Well, how were they—"

"And we don't yet know exactly how they were killed either. Could be an odd accident, could be . . . anything. We'll know more later."

Susan's heart was racing, not with fear but some

sort of excited curiosity. Suddenly, she half-imagined her never-seen neighbors having died in some gory mess, with police outlines taped around their fallen bodies. But she had no clue what might've kindled such a morbid idea.

"And when you overheard them talking in the balcony, do you recall what they were talking about? Might it have been anything unusual?"

Suddenly, she regained her focus. "Actually, since you asked, both of them did make remarks back and forth that were anti-Semitic."

Spence's brow rose over his notebook. "That's something I don't hear every day. Do you remember anything verbatim?"

She let her thought reach back. "I'm not really sure. Jews this, kikes that. Something about a 'Jew' boss who should've given the man a promotion, but I guess a woman got it instead. I'm sorry, that's about all I can remember."

Spence nodded and continued scribbling; Susan used this brief time to visually inspect the man, and immediately thought, *Wow, what a fuckin' stud. Huge and all fuckin' muscle.* One glance and she thought, *Damn it, Susan! You dirty girl!* as a liberal glance showed her a crotch with a whole lot of something in it. Then the convoluting idea sniped at her, *Yeah, I'd fuck this guy in a heartbeat. He can beat up my pussy like a flank steak at Wok'N'Roll. Shit on Jake* . . . Then she winced to herself, astonished. *What the hell is wrong with me? I NEVER think things like that!* The exceptional orgasm she'd had earlier, thanks to the clay dildo, definitely left an impression that she wasn't used to.

It also just occurred to her that as she stood in front of Spence, her robe—a sheer one, at that—was open a wee bit too much to be appropriate. *Shit!* She pulled it closer together very quickly, hoping he hadn't noticed. But even the subtle friction of this action titillated her nipples to a delicious tingle, and she even felt a definite spark right between her legs. *This is fucked up. I feel like a bitch in heat right now.*

"I guess that's about it, Ms. Knispel," Spence said.

"Please call me Susan," she said unconsciously.

"Of course, Susan, and please know that you have my deepest condolences regarding the passing of your uncle."

"Thank you."

"Here's my card . . . " he set it on the mantle beside him, "in case anything pertinent might come to mind. Oh, and may I trouble you for your phone number? In case any more questions arise as the investigation ensues?"

"It's no trouble at all," she said and gave it to him, but a silly, half-hearted thought wondered if he might really be putting the make on her, that he might call her and ask her out. Then: *Shut up, you dipsy idiot. I'm like a fuckin' old maid. That big meat-pile wouldn't fuck my worn-out forty-year-old ass with a ten-foot pole.*

Spence closed his notebook, then stalled rather sheepishly. "And . . . I'm terribly sorry to ask, but do you mind if I use your restroom? I'd use the Wittmans' but, well, it could turn out to be a crime scene, and . . . "

"Go right ahead . . . " She pointed behind her down the hall. "Last door on the right."

When the huge man moved past her, she couldn't help but raise a brow at the sight of his upper arms. His biceps were so big they'd stretch the fabric if he flexed them. *This big ox must pump motherfuckin' iron for hours a day . . .*

Inadvertently, her eyes followed him down the hall. One block of light came out on the carpet, from Uncle Petr's workroom. She must have left the light on earlier when she was—

Holy FUCK!

A jolt shocked through her.

Earlier. When she was masturbating spread-legged and cringing on the fucking floor with the big clay dildo!

Spence had stopped, curiously poised for a moment, and was looking into the workroom.

Susan stood frozen. *You've gotta be fucking SHITTING me! Did I leave the fuckin' dildo on the fucking FLOOR? Please tell me I didn't!* She remembered her instant exhaustion after the cataclysmic orgasm. She remembered feeling the hot, fat, slippery dildo slowly sliding out of her and gently *thunking* on the floor. Her pussy actually squirmed as it slid out—the "afterglow," she supposed. And then?

Then she remembered falling asleep right then and there.

Never picked the damn dildo up, did I? came the thought like a dreadful moan. No. She knew she didn't. She'd left it right there on the floor as she fell asleep, and now—

Now that big cop is standing there looking at it! Fuck!

But he was gone now; he'd moved on down the hall to use the bathroom—she could even hear him *tinkling* through the door.

She was a ninny. She was a disheveled, inattentive idiot who'd just made a giant ass out of herself. The minute Spence got back to the station, oh, did *he* have a laugher to tell!

Next came the toilet's muffled flush, the sound of the faucet, and then the bathroom door, then his bulk shadow shape coming back toward her.

She was absolutely depressed now. He *must* have seen it, he *had* to have seen it. What could she possibly say to him?

She felt tiny standing there awaiting his return. "Okay. Susan. Thank you very much for your time." And then he turned and opened the front door.

"Good-good night," she peeped.

When the door closed, she put her ear to it in an instant. *Hey, guys! This is hilarious! The broad next door had a really big dildo laying on the floor!*

But she heard no such thing, no laughter, nor any further voices.

Her robe flew open when she spun around and dashed barefoot down the hall. She grabbed the edge of the door to Uncle Petr's workroom, leaned in, and stared.

The dildo was not on the floor. In fact, it wasn't anywhere to be seen.

+ —— ❖ —— +

She'd tried to go to bed (after all, it was past four in the morning now) but the effort was unsuccessful, which was no wonder . . . *My next-door neighbors were KILLED earlier* . . . Spence had used the word *killed,* not *murdered.* However, he hadn't ruled the latter out. *This is fucked up,* she thought, curled up in bed with moonlight slanting down on her. *Why didn't Spence tell me how they were killed?* If it wasn't murder, then it must be an accident, right? Two people? In the same place, the same time? Maybe there would be more information tomorrow on the news . . .

And then came the matter of the dildo. *I KNOW I didn't pick it up after I came. I fell asleep on the fucking floor right away!* She'd searched the workroom top to bottom after Spence had left. She'd looked under the couch, under every table, behind every shelf. Nothing.

Bored now, but still wide awake, she got out of bed, pulled on her robe, and walked back to the balcony to smoke. There she noticed the sliding door slightly ajar. *Big deal. I forgot to close it earlier.* The parking lot below was pin-drop silent; it brought an eerie but content impression. *Oh, look,* she thought, when she lit a cigarette and noticed a police cruiser sitting in the corner. *Maybe Spence posted him there,* came the stray thought. *To PROTECT me! In case it WAS a murder!*

But that was nonsense. It was just a formality to post a cop following an unexplained incident. She frowned out toward the car. *Fuckin' guy is probably asleep anyway . . .*

Eventually, she put out her cigarette and drifted back inside. She wasn't tired, but she didn't feel like doing anything. *Don't wanna watch TV, don't feel like drinking . . .* Too much adrenalin was buzzing through her veins, a leftover from the day's weird excitement. Without any forethought, she found herself staring at Uncle Petr's pictures again on the mantle: mostly places in Prague decades ago, some in black and white. One photo was that of an old, tall synagogue; a very young Uncle Petr stood near the arched doorway, along with another youngish man who seemed to be missing an ear. And here was another pic of Petr with the same man, both older and both laughing on a small boat, drinking big bottles of beer and tending to fishing poles. Susan remembered her mother telling her once that Uncle Petr might be gay. *I wonder if this one-eared man was Uncle Petr's lover?* the thought drifted. *Oh, well . . . I just hope he was happy.* In all the years she'd known him, he'd always lived alone, working constantly on his pottery.

I hope you're in Heaven, she thought sadly to the photos.

The entire business with the neighbors dying still made her feel antsy; she thought about calling Jake, to tell him; but then, he'd always warned her not to call him at work, said he wasn't allowed to take personal calls. *Well fuck that,* she determined. *I'm his girlfriend, the neighbors just got killed, and I'm scared.* So she picked up her phone, was just about to dial when the phone started ringing in her hand. *Jeez!* Her heart leapt from the start. She thought sure it was Jake but—

No. The screen read METRO POLICE—ID O8. *What the . . .* "Hello . . . "

"Miss—er, Susan, this is Deputy Chief Spence again." Spence's voice sounded hollow, a bit shaky. "Did you tell me earlier that a man named Jake Radley was a person you were involved with?"

Susan's mental brakes screeched. *Am, not were* . . . "That's right, he's my boyfriend. Is something wrong?"

The following pause stretched like taffy. "I'm terribly sorry to have to tell you this, especially over the phone, but . . . Jake Radley was found dead in his car in the back lot of Villar's Warehouse."

It was probably just a few seconds that Susan stared into a block of empty space in her mind, but it seemed like hours. She just stood there with her mouth open. The words had sunk in, but no reaction surfaced. *Jake,* was all she thought. *Dead? Is that what he said?* Spence continued to talk distantly over the phone, yet his words weren't registering.

"Susan? Are you there? I realize what a shock this must be for you—"

"Yes, I'm here . . . "

"Fortunately, it won't be necessary for you to come to the morgue and ID the body; his boss already did that. But I will need to talk to you again, if you don't mind. When would be a convenient time? Or should I ask again in a few days?"

Susan's voice sounded echoic for some reason. "You can come now," she droned and hung up.

Her brain seemed to tick as she walked about the condo, the truth sinking in. *Jake's dead.* It seemed as if she couldn't close her eyes for several minutes as she pulled on a pair of jeans and a blouse.

It was still dark outside when the loud knock came at the front door. Spence looked even bigger on this second meeting, huge in his neat suit and meticulous haircut. But he had the eyes of a man in sheer mental disarray.

"You have my deepest condolences regarding the death of your boyfriend."

Susan had to look up at him. "What was the cause of death?"

"Well, that hasn't been officially declared yet, nor has the cause of death on your two neighbors." Spence seemed to wince at his thoughts. "The only word I can think of to describe this situation is 'uncanny.'"

"I still don't understand how . . . "

"It's been proposed that the Wittmans next door both died from some peculiar animal attack, and your boyfriend, Jake Radley, seems to have died similarly, several miles away."

"*What?*" Susan exclaimed. She was finally out of her daze, the truth hammering home. Jake was *dead*. She'd seen him only hours ago. *I sucked his dick and swallowed his cum.* And now he was dead. "What is it you're not telling me?"

"Well, two things, to be honest." Spence frowned. "First, your boyfriend wasn't alone when he was killed. He was found dead in the front seat of his car, with a woman who had also been killed." Spence shook his head, as if displeased with himself. "It's especially disconcerting for me to have to inform you of this . . . "

Susan's shoulders slumped. "Terrific. Jake was cheating on me. But I'm pretty sure I knew that. I'm the kind of woman who keeps her head in the sand. Always have been."

"Yes, well, I'm afraid he *was* cheating on you. He and the woman were found only half-clothed in his car. The woman's name was Tracy Jurgen; she worked for the same security company."

Figures. Any available pussy, Susan thought. Her insecurities were dying to ask Spence how old this woman was and if she was attractive, but her self-esteem wasn't prepared to sink that low just yet. "But you said two things . . . two things you hadn't told me."

Spence nodded glumly. "Of course. The manner of death, that's the uncanny part. Autopsies of your neighbors indicated some uncharacteristic severe trauma to the esophageal and digestive tracts, hence the consideration of a bizarre animal attack. Something churned these people up on the inside, and it wasn't any kind of tool or implement because the injuries don't demonstrate evidence of any toolmarks or blades."

Susan sat down on the couch as if exhausted. "I don't understand at all."

Spence sighed. "I'll elaborate. Something seems to have burrowed its way up into Mrs. Wittman's . . . vaginal tract and churned its way up through her alimentary canal and up her esophagus and then exited through her mouth. Mr. Wittman suffered similarly: this animal—rat, possum, or whatever it is—entered his anus and tore its way out of his mouth."

Susan stared up at him, mouth hanging open. "That's-that's crazy . . . "

"I'm inclined to agree, and what's crazier still is that the exact same thing happened to your boyfriend and Miss Jurgen, only several hours later and only a few miles away." Then he looked right at her.

"And sitting right in the middle of both events," Susan deduced, "is me."

Spence popped his brows. "Well, yes, but you're in no way considered a suspect. At this point, we're confident no crimes have been committed. But you can see now why I described the situation as uncanny. I've been investigating homicides, suicides, and accidental deaths for over thirty years, and I've never encountered anything close to the weirdness and inexplicability of this."

Like before, his intense eyes scanned around; she couldn't tell if he was suspicious of something or just curious. *But what could he possibly be suspicious of?* she thought. "And your crime lab people, the experts, think that it was a *possum* or *rat* that did this? That's hard to picture."

"Indeed, it is. And I'd hardly call our crime techs *experts* on wounds inflicted by animals. We simply don't know yet."

Susan sat over the edge of the couch, contemplating. "But, seriously. An *animal?* That entered the bodies of two adults and killed them before they could fight back?"

Spence could only shake his head.

"Or is it possible that it might have been *two* of the same kind of animal, both attacking Jake and his . . . this woman . . . at the same time?"

"That's a pertinent question." Now Spence was errantly examining some of Uncle Petr's clay knickknacks on an old side table. "But the answer seems to be no. You see, there was evidence of tracks, in your boyfriend's car and also in the apartment next door."

Susan squinted. "Footprints, you mean?"

"Yes, we think so. Small, like the tracks that might

be left by a large rat. The prints were made in blood initially. The animal entered Miss Jurgen via her vagina, then exited her mouth, then moved immediately to the . . . anus . . . of Jake, burrowed up his digestive tract, then exited his mouth. The tracks clearly led between Jurgen's mouth to your boyfriend's rectum, then out his mouth, out the window, and across the warehouse until the blood on the footprints wore off. Tracks taking the same route, so to speak, were found in the Wittman's abode, only they seemed to leave the premises through the open balcony door. We can assume the animal *entered* through the same balcony door as well . . . "

Susan tried to envision that sequence of events in her mind. *It's insane. I don't think I can believe it.*

Spence's attention detached itself from the knickknacks and photos as he turned toward the sliding glass door to Susan's balcony.

The door stood open an inch or two.

"And speaking of open balcony doors . . . "

Susan was surprised. "I don't get it. I'm positive I closed that door when I came back in a little while ago."

"Or almost positive," Spence suggested. "It's easy to overlook something like that, especially since you just moved in." Spence was looking down at the door's track.

"Uh, yeah, that must be it," Susan agreed. How could she *dis*agree?

Spence pulled the door open two feet, stuck his head out, looked both ways, then reclosed and locked the door. "Unlocked doors are any policeman's occupational paranoia, I'm afraid. Even two floors up, even *a hundred* floors up, always lock your balcony door. Lock *any* door, for that matter. I'm afraid that's the age we live in."

Susan nodded at the sad truth. "I usually do lock all my doors. I guess I just forgot about that one."

"Especially given that you share a partitioned balcony with the neighboring apartment and we still don't know exactly what happened there."

The implication was clear. *Whatever got into the Wittmans' place could just as easily get in here . . .* But that still didn't explain the longshot coincidence of how the same animal that killed the Wittmans had later made its way all the way to Jake's warehouse and killed him—

—*and his girlfriend,* she grimly finished the thought, *who he was fucking.*

With that, the issue became too depressing to think about. Susan plopped down on the couch, morose, staring.

"And now that I think of it, let me check something," Spence said and retraced his steps to the sliding door. He opened it and stepped back outside.

She vaguely watched him lean over the balcony rail, look up, look down, and then appear to squint directly at the brick wall that composed the side of the building. Then the man stood there, as if in contemplation.

What the hell's he looking at? Susan wondered, but before she could reflect further, she jerked her gaze behind her at a faint pattering sound.

Pattering like, perhaps, the rapid footfalls of a small animal.

Susan was so sure of the sound that she jumped up and looked down the hall. Then—

What the fu—

Did she hear it again?

Her eyes thinned; she froze where she stood, poised, listening.

But the sound, if it had ever actually existed, was not reheard.

I'm SURE I heard that— She blinked. *Er, I think I did . . .*

She wandered back toward the living room. *Heebie-jeebies,* she thought. The psychological trauma of Jake's murder was just now sinking in—part of her still didn't quite believe it—plus the other details: the Wittmans, Jake's "girlfriend," all this sudden police presence . . . *I'm just a simple restaurant manager with a simple life . . . Fuck this . . .*

However, her recollection remained quite clear. When Susan was in junior high, she and her family lived in a mobile home at a trailer park. Every now and then, particularly at night, a rat, possum, or squirrel would scamper across the thin rubberized roof. That scampering sound was just like the sound she thought she'd heard in the uncarpeted hallway.

All she could do was shake her head. *Just my imagination,* she knew, wandering back into the living room. All these negative events hitting her all at once were sabotaging her observations. That would be true of anyone in a similar situation.

"What were you looking at outside?" she asked.

Spence had come back off the balcony and locked the door behind him. He looked flustered. "I was just trying to see how an animal like a rat or possum might be able to climb from the ground up to the Wittmans' second-story balcony. I seriously doubt they could scale the brick facade, even at the corners. I know that rats frequently climb trees and are able to walk across the power lines to rooftops of houses and apartment buildings . . . but then, how would they get down to the second-story?"

She tried to think about what he'd said, but her mind was too muddled. *Who's making the final arrangements for Jake?* she wondered in her daze. *He'd never introduced me to his parents. I don't even know where he was born. Is he going to be buried or cremated? Fuck* . . . "Do you know . . . er, won't they put in the paper if there'll be a memorial service for my boyfriend?"

Spence seemed to be squinting down at the floor now; the question caught him off guard. "Oh . . . yes, that's the usual procedure. So I'm presuming you don't know who his next of kin are?"

She shook her head. "I've got no idea, and to tell you the truth, I don't know that much about him."

"Well, I'll make some inquiries and get back to you, okay?" he offered. "And I'll keep you posted on the case. Right now, our TSD crew is at the warehouse, and then they'll be looking at the Wittmans' apartment."

Susan frowned. "TSD?"

"Our technical services people. They'll make a closer examination of the areas in question."

"Oh, okay," Susan droned.

Spence repeated his condolences and then left. When she'd shown him to the door, she couldn't help but notice more police in the hallway. *This must be a bigger deal than he's letting on,* she reasoned.

Spence disappeared into a crowd of uniformed

backs; Susan withdrew, as if shriveling up, back into her apartment. She closed and locked the door.

This *had* to be one of the worst days of her life. *Boyfriend dead. People killed next door, just one wall away from me.* And the more she thought of it, if there *was* some kind of memorial service for Jake, *I probably won't even go. And I doubt that many other people will either.* Jake was all about himself. He didn't have many friends, and in truth, he wasn't a very nice guy. *Just along for the ride, and I was the wagon. Just a piece of ass and a roof over his head.*

She couldn't have felt more dismal when she staggered into her bedroom and flopped down on the bed.

Fairly quickly, she began to doze in and out. Images of senseless dreams flushed around in her head, the oddest mental pictorials. Drab unpaved streets, apparently in some ancient city, overlooked by a high sinister fortification. Foul smoke gushed from chimneys; black soot veneered every edifice, including churches and synagogues, and wearied horses drew carts and carriages back and forth, leaving mounds of periodic excrement in the streets. The grim, stoop-shouldered denizens of this place shuffled down filthy sidewalks toward whatever sullen onus awaited them, their grimy hands clutching nameless parcels. They all wore leggings more like bandages and dirty woolen surplices. But these crowds cleared for the occasional platoons of soldiers that marched in formation, all wearing shiny steel cabasset helmets, most carrying bannered pikes, and some with matchlock muskets. When crippled beggars were unable to get out of their way, they were marched over.

In and out of this dream, Susan's mind wobbled. Eventually, she was cognizant of being awake on her bed, submerged in darkness. So she'd slept the whole day away? But even if she had, what difference did it make? Some mental specter seemed to be drawing closer to her, and after a few moments, she knew what it was: the reality. The reality she'd forgotten whilst asleep. Jake was dead. *He's never coming home,* came the groggy realization. Tears misted her eyes, but suddenly, she was smiling, smiling in the dark, like a secret. Yes, her boyfriend was dead, but he'd always been a pretty shitty boyfriend, hadn't he? She'd settled for him because he was an antidote for her loneliness and she wasn't getting any younger. And with her, he got to have his cake and eat it too: sex anytime he wanted it with her, plus God knew how many other girls, and Susan paid most of the bills. *What a shit life I handed myself,* she thought, but then she grinned again when the truth struck home. *He'll never put it in my ass again, and he's gotten his last blowjob. I've swallowed that shithead's cum for the last time. Fuck him . . .*

It wasn't like her to be this hateful and cynical. But for some reason, thinking about Jake with another woman brought a swell of erotic contemplation, but . . . why on earth would that be? At any rate, when she was next aware of herself, the room seemed even darker and she lay widely spread-legged on the bed with her jeans unfastened and her hand in her panties. The brink of climax was almost instantaneous, but as her hand worked more fervently, she couldn't quite get over the hump and make herself come. Myriad erotic images rifled through her mind, but she couldn't find the right one to go with. Jake's hard cock, poised and throbbing. That same cock slamming into her, and then slamming into another woman. Susan watching this other woman blow Jake a mile a minute, and then the other woman's mouth filling with Jake's orgasm . . . eventually, she leaned over, yanked open Susan's mouth, and let the heap of sperm slide into Susan's mouth . . .

"Fuck!" she whispered aloud.

No orgasm; she couldn't make it over the hurdle in spite of being more horny than ever. *What a rip-off,* she thought. *I guess I'm just fucked up in the head* . . . The bedroom's grainy darkness pushed down like shadow people huddled all about her, urging her to go back to sleep, and in an expenditure of time that seemed interminable, the eye of Susan's mind rematerialized back on the stinking, ancient dream-street of beggars, horse waste, and stooped-shouldered street denizens. Only this time, the street's tenor seemed charged with some unseen terror. Residents were fleeing, screaming, and still more, heavier screams sailed down the street. Children were plucked from sidewalks and whisked into their ghettoish homes. Another tide of screams arose down the street; now more squads of pike-wielding soldiers double-timed toward the commotion and around a corner. Meanwhile, the eye of Susan's dreaming mind floated down the street, and then it arrived at the corner and looked . . .

Over a dozen soldiers lay dead or close to death. Several had been de-limbed, others decapitated— either that or their heads, helmets and all, had been squashed against the brick wall. Several soldiers twitched where they lay, their pikes were rammed down their throats or rammed up their anuses. Others were strung with garlands of their own innards. A single musketeer had had his weapon wrapped around his neck, and then, somehow, his body had been divided into two pieces at the waist. The entire street was awash with blood.

This was the image in Susan's mind when she next awoke and found herself cringing in the rigors of orgasm. Each contraction of pleasure struck her like a seizure. She had no control of herself as she came; she thought she must be moaning very loudly, and at one point, she bit her tongue and shrieked. Still, wave after wave of dense, high-saturated pleasure throbbed at her loins. Eventually, she felt too wasted and exhausted to come any more, but she came more anyway; the orgasm wrung her body out like a wet rag through her spasming pussy.

Finally done, she lay breathless, eyes bulged, and near-paralyzed. At last, her brain engaged and she managed to think, *I can't fuckin' believe it. I didn't know orgasms could even BE that good.* Her eyes began to acclimate to the dark; a shard of moonlight slanted in through a gap in the curtains, drawing a line across her body, which, she noticed now, was fully unclothed. This confounded her; she couldn't remember getting out of her clothes, yet there they lay, like scraps of meat, all around her on the bed. She remembered the awful dream she'd had, slaughtered soldiers in some dark ancient alley, but then wakening to the delicious orgasm. How could her mind and body coordinate such an illogical instance?

And then she got to wondering, as she lay in the dark: what had killed those helmeted soldiers? What was her subconscious implying? There was nothing erotic about the scene of gore and dismemberment. Nevertheless, there had been some correlation, some trigger, between the ghastly scene and what was undoubtedly the most satisfying sexual release of her life.

Next, her hand inadvertently slid over her pubic hair to her still-sensitive vulva . . .

Susan gulped hard. *What in the holy fuckin' . . . ?*

Between her legs, nudged right up against her sex, was the missing clay dildo she'd made in Uncle Petr's workshop. Her fingers inspected it; it was still wet, and it felt warmer than she would expect. She must've been partly asleep when she found it hidden amongst the covers and then put it to use without conscious awareness. Strange, though, that she couldn't remember, and she couldn't remember putting it on the bed earlier. She lay back, staring up at the grainy ceiling, thinking, thinking—

Shit . . .

—and thinking some more.

She was thinking about the orgasm she'd just had, the opiate-like assault of cringing, seething pleasure. Suddenly, the scent of the clay returned, that hot, almost fleshy earthiness, and then one finger was trailing up the inflamed groove of her pussy, and then, and then . . .

Fuck it. I gotta do it again!

Her hand shot just below her sex where the clay dildo was—with every intention of picking it up and teasing it back into herself—but—

Now wait just one fuckin' minute . . .

Susan went rigid on the bed. The dildo was no longer between her legs where it had undoubtedly been just a moment ago.

She sat up, turned on the bedside light, leaned over, patted all around the bed. She visually and manually combed every inch of the covers, then hopped off and scanned the floor in case the dildo had rolled off. But . . . no dildo was to be seen. Which was impossible because she'd just touched it. *I think there's something really WRONG about this place,* she thought, repeating her search. Where could it have gone? The mystery was particularly vexing because her hormones were suddenly raging again, and she *really, really* wanted to use it. Susan stood there, brazenly naked, hands on hips, frowning as her eyes combed the bedroom floor. She even looked under the bed, and there was nothing.

Well, I KNOW it was here, she reasserted. *It didn't just get up and walk away . . .*

Perhaps that cliched observation was appropriate, because as she was standing back up, she thought she heard—

No way . . .

It was a sound like a rapid *patter,* a tiny but deliberate and unmistakable sound as of, say, a sizable rodent. Not here in the carpeted bedroom but out in the uncarpeted hallway.

Damn it! I KNOW I heard that!

She dashed naked to the bedroom doorway, looked left toward the living room, saw nothing, then looked right farther down the hall, and—

Her mouth fell open.

A movement had snagged her eyes, down on the floor just at the opening of Uncle Petr's workroom, and then whatever it had been disappeared into the room.

"What the fuck?"

But what had it been? The image that had registered in her eyes didn't at all seem rodent-like, but then . . . it didn't seem to remind her of anything familiar. Just a dark blur, perhaps a foot high. *What the hell WAS that?* she wondered in an alarming anxiety. She did feel a wisp of fear, however, but why should she fear something so small? Or . . .

Had she even really seen it?

Did I imagine it? she tried to suggest to herself, but the answer shot back: *No! I really HEARD that pattering sound, and I really SAW that little . . . whatever it was!*

She took one step forward, then another, then stopped. A subtle draft made her naked skin tingle, and the—

She sniffed.

And there was that scent again, that earthy mud-like organic aroma that kindled her sexual sensibilities; in fact, even as scant as the scent was, she felt a dense erotic pulse between her leg and a welling of hot moisture. *This is crazy! I'm horny again! Too much fucked up shit has happened here way too fuckin' fast!* She had to will herself not to press her finger against her clitoris.

Determined to get to the bottom of all this, she took another step forward toward the workroom door—

BAM-BAM-BAM-BAM-BAM!

Susan brought a hand to her heart and shrieked. *Who the FUCK is pounding on my door!* The surprise disoriented her. She stood ludicrously poised in the hall, naked, jerking her gaze between the workroom door and the foyer.

BAM-BAM-BAM-BAM-BAM!

Who could it be? And what time was it? She rushed back to the bedroom and clumsily pulled on her clothes. The clock told her it was just past nine p.m. *It must be Spence at the door; maybe he found out more information . . .* She immediately assumed it must be Spence again and he wanted to tell her something.

She hurried to the front door and opened it.

A mild shock struck her, for it wasn't Spence who'd been knocking.

Who the hell . . .

An elderly man, balding with white hair and very skinny, faced her now. He had to be in his mid-'70s. And there was one other very noticeable detail: he was missing his right ear.

The guy in the photo, on the boat with Uncle Petr . . .

But much, much older now.

His bright blue eyes twinkled in recognition. And in a sharp Czech accent, he pronounced. "Ah, yes, you are Zuzanka. I once meet you when you were little child. I am Andrej. Petr was my best friend. We come here together long time ago as young men, from Praha."

She understood the "Zuzanka," which was one way to say Susan in Czech; Uncle Petr had called her the same thing. And he was obviously for real, obviously the same man in the photo. "Please come in," she said.

When she let him in, the old man paused, looking around, half-sad and half-satisfied. "Yes, this place bring back fine memories," he said. "Petr and I, we drink many beers here and talk about the good times back in Praha. In fact," he raised a finger, "I be right back," and went to the kitchen and opened the refrigerator. In a moment, he returned with a big can of beer.

Help yourself, why don't you? Susan thought.

But now, this man—Andrej—was perusing the photos of the mantle, just as Spence had earlier. "World was so different back then," Andrej reflected. "Different in good ways but also in bad. You see this ear?" he asked, pointing to a hole in the right side of his head. "This ear here, er, I mean where ear used to be?"

"Um . . . yes."

"Was back in sixty-eight when that happen, during the Revolution—ah! Petr and me, we were so young. Eighteen, nineteen. And it was my people, they try to revolt against Soviets and throw them out. Was one Russian soldier, he was the devil who cut off my ear, and I won't say what else it was he do to me, but your brave uncle—God bless him—he take that Russian's bayonet and stick it, well, I won't tell you what he do. Petr save my life that day. But—ah—all went bad. The Soviets killed many of us and imprison hundreds."

"Wow, that's quite a story," Susan said, "and, believe me, I very much appreciate you being friends with my uncle, but . . . is there anything I can do for you?"

The old man looked confused. "Vas?"

"Um . . . why are you here?"

The old man stared, paused, then gusted a laugh. "Ah! Of course! You want reason for me coming here—yes! Well, I tell you it is just to check on something that Petr would want me to check, but I sure it is nothing. I see on news some people were killed in this building—"

He'd pronounced "killed" as *keeled*.

"Yes, yes, the neighbors just next door were killed," Susan exclaimed. "I didn't know it had made the news already. What else did they say?"

The old man's pull on the beer emptied half the can. "They say they think an animal or something but . . . "

"But what?" she blurted.

"There is something, probably nothing, but something I must check because Petr would want it." And then he turned quickly and made down the hall.

Susan followed him, perturbed. *Damn, this guy acts like he owns the place!*

Andrej had bolted directly into Petr's workroom, and he was already down on his knees by the time Susan came in. "What the hell!"

He knew exactly what he was looking for: he pulled out the one box under the table that Susan was most familiar with. She easily noted the magic-markered word VLTAVA scrawled on the wooden lid. "Probably nothing, probably nothing," Andrej was saying under his breath, but his demeanor changed when he pulled open the squeaky wooden lid and stared down. The large parcel of pallid grayish-brownish clay remained wrapped in clear plastic, which Andrej immediately began to unwrap, until the surface of the bare clay was revealed. Also revealed, of course, was the big divot Susan had previously carved out of it with the chisel.

The old man quickly looked up, his expression suggesting something like trepidation tinged by outrage. "Vas? Petr did not make this hole. Someone take some clay from this box! Was it you?"

Susan's lower lip quivered. All she could do was look back at him, wide-eyed.

"It must be you!" he yelled. "Petr would not take out this clay! Why? Why you take clay from this box?"

At once, Susan felt persecuted, nervous, and embarrassed. "I—"

"Why!"

Fuck! What could she say? "All right, damn it! I made a dildo out of it!"

Andrej's old face warped. "A *deel-doe?* You mean like sex toy women use to stick in thereselves?"

Her face turned beet red. "Yes! So what?"

He jabbed a finger down at the divot. "You make deel-doe with this clay? This clay here?"

"Yes!" she shrieked, furious. What a thing to have to admit!

Andrej, still on his knees before the opened box, put his face in his hands and moaned. "Oh, no, oh no! What you have done you have no idea . . . "

Now her anger was bubbling over her embarrassment. "Big deal, damn you! I made a fake dick out of a lump of clay! That's not a crime!"

He gave her the grimmest look. "Bůh v nebi . . . Is crime against rabbinic law. Is crime against the Code of the Holy Maharal and the Kabbalah!" He put his hand on the open box. "This clay is not just any clay! Is clay from Vltava River in Praha, same clay used by

Rabbi Loew hundreds of years ago to make the Golem of Prague! You must know of Golem of Prague!"

"I don't know what you're talking about!" Susan shouted back.

"Oh, God! How can you be a Jew and not know about Golem?" moaned the old man.

By now, Susan was so flustered she couldn't entertain a linear thought. *What the fuck is this old nutjob doing here!* "Look, mister, I don't know what's with you and all this shit about the clay, but I want you out of here! Right now!"

"Oh, no." Andrej said gravely. "I cannot leave until we find it."

"Find *what?* My dildo?"

He looked up pleadingly. "Zuzanka, I beg you to understand. That thing you make with this clay is no deel-doe! It's a golem. It's like a genie from a magic lamp. Once you stick it in yourself, you-you-you *invoke* it. To thank you for giving it life, it do your bidding. You become its master."

"It's a *dildo,* you idiot!" she bellowed. "Not a genie!"

Andrej stood up in haste. "We must find it right now. I must deactivate it before it kill again! Where is your deeldoe?"

I can't believe this is happening! "It was right here on the bed a minute ago, but now it's not. It's disappeared a few times."

Andrej looked around desperately. "You hear maybe any noise? Any strange noise?"

"Like what?"

"Like maybe little feet running?"

Susan stared back at the man. *Shit . . .* "Well, yes.

Just before you knocked. It sounded like a small animal running."

"Where did it run?"

Susan gulped. "Right in here. From the bedroom to here—"

Andrej immediately got back down on his knees and began searching the room. "We must find this! You must help me!"

Before she could give her actions much thought, Susan was about to get on her knees as well, but—

Someone started knocking loud on the door. *Oh, fuck me! It might be Spence again.* "Listen!" she barked. "Don't you dare say a word about deeldoes or golems!" and then she ran to the front door.

Spence was indeed the knocker. "Come in," she said, suspecting he had more information murders, killings, and whatever they were. But he was holding some bulky device that looked like a portable lamp.

"Once again, I apologize for intruding," he said and entered. "We discovered something of interest next door at the Wittmans', and I'd like to ask your permission to perform a quick forensic scan in your apartment."

Forensic scan, she thought blankly. "Oh, you mean, like, fingerprints?"

"More like footprints, if anything," he said. He set the lamp-looking device on the table and explained. "This is a multi-wavelength scan light. It's tunable for nineteen light wavelengths from ultraviolet to normal visible light, all the way to infrared at eight hundred and thirty nm. You've probably seen UV lights on crime shows, but this adds a more elaborate dimension. Variations of certain frequencies of light can have visible effects on certain kinds of evidence. It can cause evidence to darken or fluoresce when it would be otherwise invisible."

Susan wasn't focusing; she was too worried about Andrej loping out and spouting off about magic Clay from Prague and dildos. "Yes, I think I know what you mean, and you can go ahead and use that if you want."

Spence got right to work. He turned off all the lights in the kitchen and living room and then clicked on his machine. First, he roved it around the kitchen floor, but this revealed nothing of interest: dust and tiny flecks of things that appeared to glow a very faint aquamarine. Then Spence turned the device toward the carpeted living room.

"Wow! What's all that?"

Spence stopped, waving the lamp back and forth. With every sweep, more spots began to fluoresce, only these spots weren't flecks, they were almost an inch long, ovalish in shape.

What the fuck?

"See?" Spence said. "Looks like little footprints, doesn't it? These were all over the Wittmans' apartment too, on the living room floor, on the balcony, and on the bed where they were killed." Next, he walked to the sliding door. "Um-hmm . . . "

Several lines of the glowing prints led to and from the door, and she could even see some outside on the balcony.

"This is crazy," Susan exclaimed. "These are footprints of the thing that killed the neighbors and also Jake and his girlfriend?"

"It seems likely."

Spence went out on the balcony, roving his

forensic lamp around. When he returned several moments later, his eyes were wide. "You'll find this hard to believe, but I just found evidence of more tracks . . . going up and down the side of the building to this balcony."

Susan had to admit that what was hard to believe a day ago was becoming very believable now. *Magic clay? Occult clay? Do I really believe that?* "So, you mean that whatever this animal is, it *scaled* up the bricks of this building?"

They traded solemn glances.

"It's beginning to look that way," he said, but he was clearly becoming more flustered by the growing entails of this case.

What the fuck is really going on? Susan thought and just then—

The faint pattering sound she'd heard earlier sounded again.

"Please tell me you heard that!" Susan said.

Spence's mouth hung open. "I heard it."

And next, bold as brass, the thing, the mystery, the instigator of the noise finally showed itself. In fact, it ran out of the hallway, then veered between Spence and Susan, cut across the living room carpet, and disappeared under the couch.

Susan shrieked.

Spence said, "Holy motherfuckin' *shit* . . . "

"So you saw that, right?"

"I-I can't deny it," the policeman stammered. "What did you see? Tell me, and I'll tell you what *I* saw."

Susan's mental gears churned. What had it been? "I'll tell you what I *didn't* see. I didn't see a rat or any kind of rodent. It was—I don't know—it was almost like a brown blob with things maybe like arms and legs. It was like a doll, a crude doll, about a foot high." She blinked at her own words. "But that's impossible. That's insane . . . right?"

Spence pinched the bridge of his nose. "That's exactly what I saw as well."

They stared at each other in silent bewilderment, then Spence said, "What the hell *was* that thing?"

The answer thundered from another voice: "Was a golem, I tell you! Made living from the sacred laws of Kabbalah and given body by power of Vltava clay! It was a *golem!*"

Oh, shit, Susan thought.

Of course, it was the old and teetering Andrej who'd just walked in on the conversation. Susan quickly introduced the two, then Susan said, "Did you see it too?"

"I see it, oh, yes!" snapped the old man. "And we must stop it!"

Spence's great height seemed to collapse like a demolitioned building when he sat down on a chair. He let out a long, weary sigh, then looked up at Andrej. "And you said this thing is a golem?"

"Yes!" Andrej's voice cracked. "Made from clay, just as *we* were made of clay by God's hand, from the clay and the dust which we all will return to! Through the holy magic of the Kabbalah, a golem can be made to serve the just and destroy all enemies of God!" Andrej's cracking voice and volume made his rant seem even more crackpot. "The golem is a minister of God's vengeance!"

"Oh, boy," Spence muttered under his breath. "That's a little hard to believe, sir."

Andrej jabbed his finger forward. "But you *just* see it! You see it run across floor!"

Spence paused on a thought. "I did see something, sir. I admit that. And it was pretty—"

"Fucked up," Susan said. "I know this sounds crazy but . . . I think it might be true."

"Of *course* is true!" Andrej bellowed and chugged more beer.

"I remember mythology class in college," Spence said. "As I recall, golems are huge things bigger than men. That little thing we just saw was doll-sized."

Andrej shrugged his shoulders. "Golem can be any size you make it."

"And who made this one?"

Oh, no, Susan thought.

Andrej looked right over at Susan.

"*I* made it," she admitted, frowning at herself. "My Uncle Petr was a potter, and when he died, he left me this place and everything in it. In his workroom, there's a bunch of clay. Most of it's commercial, but one box is full of, well, of . . . "

"Of *what?*"

"Of . . . *special* clay," Susan replied without much confidence.

Andrej kept pointing his finger, his old voice booming: "Is *Vltava* clay! Was made special by the Maharal, Judah ben Loew, back in fifteen hundreds, was made *magic!*"

Spence rubbed his face in his hands again. "Okaaaay . . . "

"This guy, way back when," Susan began, "he was a rabbi and Jewish mystic. In Prague, the Jews were confined to a ghetto, and they were persecuted by the emperor's soldiers. Women and children were raped and murdered, men were slaughtered, like, by the thousands. So Rabbi Loew enchanted the clay in the Vltava River and made a golem. And . . . the thing came to life and, well, kicked serious ass. It tore the shit out of any soldiers it came in contact with." Susan paused grimly, remembered her dream fragment, the piles of headless or dismembered soldiers, the waves of screams like surf, the entire street shiny with blood. "It was unstoppable. It couldn't be hurt. All it could do was kill all enemies of the Jews."

Was this Andrej's second beer or third? He was already copping a big buzz. "Yes! It tear the men apart! It take out their insides and throw it on street. So the emperor come to Judah ben Loew and beg him to make golem stop, and in return, he will leave Jews alone. The rabbi agrees but . . . is too late! The golem become so enraged by the crimes against the Jews that its violence grow beyond the control of Rabbi Judah! The golem attack Prague Castle, break down walls, and search for emperor, killing everyone in its path. But at last minute, the rabbi say a spell from the Kabbalah that make golem go asleep, and then he take golem apart and hide the pieces in the attic of the Altneushul!"

"The what?" Spence wearily asked.

"The synagogue," Susan said. "And he hid the pieces of clay up in the attic; in all that time since then, the pieces of the golem have never been found. And, well, what you need to understand is that there's a big box of that same stuff sitting in my dead uncle's workroom right now."

It was only the work of a moment before the trio

had entered the workroom and Susan was hauling out the big wooden box of brownish, grayish clay. "There it is," she said; she opened the lid, releasing the earthy, exotic scent. "There's the clay—"

"Not just any clay!" Andrej interrupted again. "Is *Vltava* clay, the clay that—"

"Yeah, yeah, I get it," Spence snapped, then his gaze turned piercing, and he stared right at Susan. "And *you* used it to make *another* golem? Do I have that right?"

Susan let out a deep breath; she felt as though she were shrinking. "I . . . I didn't make a golem—"

But Andrej was chuckling now. "No! She no make golem! She make *deel-doe!*"

You drunken old fuck! I ought to kick you right in your ancient balls, you big mouthed grandpa-looking stick!

Spence squinted at her. "I didn't understand him. You made *what?*"

Susan didn't want even to consider how red her face was now turning. She simply said it, "I made a dildo."

Andrej continued cackling. "Yes! Zuzanka use the Vltava clay to make *dildo!* And then she stick it in her woman-place!"

At this, even Spence had to crack a smile and release a few chuckles.

"Oh, you too?" she snapped. *Fuck it! Whatever happened to privacy?* "Yeah, yeah, since you *must* know, I was horny and I couldn't remember which moving box my vibrator was in, and my fuckin' boyfriend was at work boffing some tramp, and now he's dead, and, to be honest, I don't really care that much because he was a free-loader, liar, and asshole, so, yes! I made a *fuckin' dildo* with the clay, and I used it! For fuck's sake, that's not a crime . . . "

"No, of course it's not," Spence said, but then the grin reappeared. "But you have to admit, it's kind of funny . . . "

"Fuck off! You can both kiss my ass!"

Spence was clearly at odds with the situation. From the instant Susan had met him, he'd struck her as a man always in control and incapable of being frustrated.

But not now.

"Let's forget about the dildo. I'm finding it impossible to compartmentalize the things that have happened here lately. But I'm pretty certain that I don't believe in golems or any other aspect of the supernatural."

"If it's not a golem, then explain how four people were killed by something crawling through their insides and coming out their mouths," Susan challenged him. "Explain that thing we just saw run across the floor and go under the couch."

Andrej seemed to titter in the background while Spence stared outward.

"See? Big American policeman no like it when his beliefs are challenged," Andrej said in obvious amusement. "Golem is here, right now, and he know it. And his big American policeman gun will do him no good, he-he-he . . . "

"We'll see about that," Spence said and then reached into his suit jacket and pulled out the biggest revolver Susan had ever seen, sparkling chrome, so big it was nearly a caricature. The barrel had to be ten inches long.

"Big gun, bigger gun," Andrej went on, slugging more beer. "Big policeman, bigger policeman—bah! All this mean nothing to a golem."

"Sir, please pardon my acumen," Spence said, "but before you're too shit-faced to be of any use at all, would you please pull the couch away from the wall?"

Andrej huffed arrogantly. "Ah, big policeman need *old man* to do his job, huh?"

"For dick's sake," Susan said, exasperated. "I'll do it," and she grabbed the couch end and pulled, swinging it away from the wall in a great sweep.

Spence stood flummoxed, his huge pistol pointing down. "Damn it. No golem. I must be nuts . . . "

Susan leaned over the couch back, peering at the wall. For a brief moment, she was aware that if Spence had been looking at her, he would've gotten a bird's eye view of her bare breasts showing in the "hang-down" of her blouse, and this prospect vaguely titillated her, but—*Shit*. He was glancing behind the couch, not at her. *Damn, man. What kind of cop are you? Bare tits practically in your face and you don't even notice . . .* "But look," she said. "There *is* something, isn't there? What is that?"

Spence squinted, nodding curiously. "Yeah. Is it a small wall panel of some sort?"

Andrej shuffled around with his beer, took another chug, then looked down. "Ah, just as I think. Golem escaped."

"It couldn't have escaped," Susan snapped. "We've all been standing here the whole time."

"We would've seen it," Spence added.

Andrej flipped his hand dismissively. "No, no.

Golem escape through *that*," and he pointed at the irregularity Susan had noticed.

She and Spence both squatted down to look more closely. Behind the couch, down near the baseboard, there was what looked like a rough square shape, like something drawn directly on the wall.

"Is a *průchod,* a *svatý* průchod," Andrej informed them. "Is from old Jewish magic. Is like a doorway that Golem draw on wall with finger and use to escape."

"That's a crock of shit," Susan said, glaring at the old man. "You telling us that a fuckin' clay doll drew that square, opened it like a door, and went through?"

"Is exactly what I'm saying to you. Naturally, a younger American woman and big policeman won't believe such things, but I tell you, it's true. A golem know very powerful magic."

Now Spence addressed Andrej. He didn't seem quite as incredulous as Susan. "So, you're saying that it went through that door and is now in the wall or in the next room?"

Andrej's face creased up in objection. "Bah! No! Not next room! It use průchod to go to another place—a *nether*-place. Is like—"

"Another dimension?" Spence said.

"Yes! Like you just say. Through the průchod, to the other place where it can hide."

"That's the dumbest bunch of shit I've ever heard," Susan said.

But Spence parted from them, then returned a moment later with his clunky forensic lamp. "Let's just see . . ."

He knelt in the space between the floor and the

pushed-out couch, then clicked on the lamp. Instantly, the tiny luminous spots of aquamarine eerily appeared.

"I don't believe it," Susan said.

The glowing prints led straight to the baseboard where the square had been drawn and then ended. As if the thing had walked straight into the wall.

"There. Now you see," Andrej said in a huff. "Now you believe old man from Praha. And what is bad is that Golem can come back out through průchod *any time it wants*. To kill again." He'd again pronounced the word "kill" as *keel*.

"So what do we do?" Spence said, aggravated. "Can we wipe off the square, the průchod? Or maybe nail a board over it?"

"Yeah," Susan said. "Like a mouse hole."

Andrej shook his head, chuckling. "Silly American people. There is nothing *you* can do except thank God that I am here." He finished his beer. "Now bring me another can of beer while I make special preparations. Oh, and bring me also a toothpick," and then he hobbled down the hallway and turned into Uncle Petr's workroom.

A beer and a toothpick. Great. Susan looked at Spence. "So we're okay with this? The nutty old man says there's a golem behind the wall, hiding in another dimension or some shit . . . and we're buying that? We're believing that?"

Spence looked eroded by weariness. "Shit, I don't know . . . yeah, I guess. Why the fuck not?"

"At least it can't hurt to wait and see what happens," Susan offered.

When she returned from the kitchen with another

beer—and a toothpick—Andrej was just returning himself. He was holding something in his palm that appeared to be a blob of clay the size of a cherry tomato.

"You Americans, yes, all you know is your Facebooks and your silly phones that take selfies and your machines that talk to you and turn on the lights or coffee maker. Bah! Such stupid things is the magic of the modern age, but this," he held up the blob of clay, "*this* is real magic, ancient Kabbalah magic that go back in history thousands of years." The old man smiled conceitedly. "Now Andrej show you what magic really is!"

He walked behind the couch, then awkwardly got on his knees where the průchod had been inscribed on the drywall. From this angle, Susan couldn't really see what he was doing, and eventually, he stuck his crabbed hand out and said, "Give me toothpick."

Susan did so, frowning, after which Andrej seemed to hunch over and busy himself for several minutes. She and Spence traded silent looks of bafflement, but then Susan—never known for a hefty attention span—caught her gaze wandering up and down his massive, broad-shouldered body. *Damn, I'd like to fuck him. I wonder if I've got a shot?* As big as he was, and as small as *she* was, she could picture him squashing her flat, twisting her up like a Gumby. *Please, please! Use me for a fuck dummy! My life's dull as shit!*

When her preposterous muse evaporated, Andrej was already standing back up, wiping off his hands, and drinking more beer. "There. Now all is back to good. Golem is trapped and can never get out."

"Why?" Susan asked. "What did you do?"

"I'd be interested in hearing that myself," Spence said.

Andrej acted nonchalant. "I stick piece of Vltava clay in middle of průchod and then use toothpick to write word on it."

"What word?" Susan smirked.

"Special magic Kabbalah word about which you know nothing and *need* to know nothing. Is a *seal*. It will keep golem sealed in forever."

"In other words," Spence guessed, "you closed off the průchod, like locking a door."

"Yes, big American policeman," Andrej affirmed. "That is perfect way to describe. Golem is locked in and can't get out."

A long pause floated before them all.

Susan said, "So what next?"

"What next, Zuzanka asks? Well, I tell you. First, you thank me for probably saving your lifes. Then, I leave and go to bingo hall. And you two? You push that couch back against wall and forget all about golem. And never, ever touch the průchod or the seal. Never go near it, never show to anyone, never think about it. You will please understand this. Is very important. And now," he chugged the rest of the beer, "I go."

Susan sighed. "Okay, well. Thank you, Andrej."

"Yes, thank you, sir," Spence said.

"Yes, yes, and goodbye to you both. Zuzanka, I hope we see each other again—oh, yes, and that big box of Vltava clay in Petr's room? You leave it alone for rest of life. Never touch it, never even look at it again, and . . . *and* . . .

Don't you dare say it, you old fuck! Susan thought.

" . . . never make dildo again! Ever!"

Susan's face reddened once more. Naturally, he'd pronounced "dildo" as *deel-doe.*

Andrej wobbled toward the door. "And you too, big giant American policeman. Goodbye to you."

Spence and Susan's mouths hung open as they watched him leave.

"Fuck," Spence said.

"So that's it?" Susan asked. "He sticks a piece of clay on the wall and presto, problem solved? The murder spree is over?"

"It appears so . . . "

Spence walked behind the couch and crouched down; Susan followed him and watched as he produced a tiny penlight and applied its beam to the area of the pruchod. Indeed, that little ball of clay had been pressed into the square outline and was now stuck to the wall. A tiny etching had been inscribed on it—no doubt by Andrej and his toothpick.

"I guess that's the magic word," Spence said.

Susan squinted and could see it, what looked like a string of warped, upside-down U's, several B's either backward or turned ninety degrees, and several warped A's with weird accents.

"Is that Hebrew?" Spence asked.

"I don't know. That shows you how good a Jew I am. But it looks like it might be."

Spence stood back up. "Well, then . . . I guess that's good enough for me. If it's all bullshit, then we'll find out soon enough. But as of this minute, as far as

I'm concerned, this case is closed and the victims were killed by wild animal attacks."

Susan shrugged. "Sounds good to me, I guess."

Spence pushed the couch back against the wall. "And now, Susan, I'm sending all those cops home, and I'll be on my way."

Shit . . . Her eyes took in one last look at him. "But, wait . . . There's a great Cantonese place around the corner. Let's go. My treat."

He turned with his hand on the doorknob. "That's very generous to offer, but I'm bushed, and I need to get home to my husband."

All of Susan's thoughts screeched to a halt. "Oh, um, yes, of course . . . "

"Have a good night," he said cheerily and then left.

It's one kick in the ass after another, she thought after the door closed. *That big muscle-rack's got a HUSBAND. I just can't win.*

As the twilight deepened, she stood out on the balcony sipping wine and watching all the police and technicians pack up and drive away. In no long time, the parking lot was back to its usual pin-drop silence. She could see the moon and the stars glittering. But she couldn't help but wonder how she was going to reckon all that had happened. Boyfriend dead? Neighbors murdered? An ancient monster imprisoned behind the wall? *Fuck it. Why worry about stuff I can't do anything about?* Under the circumstances, this seemed the most practical way to deal with it all. And for whatever reason, she felt very content right now and confident that if the golem really did exist, it would stay locked behind that wall.

So everything's good! she thought in a burst of happiness.

But the happiness quickly petered out. She meandered back inside, poured more wine, and realized what the problem was; she knew why she felt suddenly deprived.

She was still extremely horny . . .

That fuckin' clay dildo gave me the best orgasms of my life, but now it's all over. I can never make another one. Fuck!

Susan turned all the lights up and began tearing into all those moving boxes. She'd find her vibrator if it took all night.

MACHO-MAN 3000

Ondřej Kocáb

translated by Kateřina Cukrová

"**SO, WHAT DO** you have for me this time?"

Erwin went without saying a word to the blanket covering an object the body height of a well-built man. Before the blanket touched the floor, it became apparent that it was really a male body hidden under it. Completely naked and well-defined. It looked absently into space.

Victoria clung for a short time to the manhood of the naked man and then turned her attention back to the Erwin with raised eyebrow. "Well? I'm waiting."

"As you surely know, our department performs miracles in the field of robotics. We are able to—"

"Cut the crap and make your point."

"Okay, little sister," said with the same professional smile, "it reached my ears that you have some . . . can we call it problems?"

Her lips tightened into a thin line, and her cheeks turned slightly purple.

"I don't know what you're talking about."

"I think that you know. What about that one, what was his name . . . Alex? As I know he ran away so fast that he didn't manage to get dressed. Is that true?"

"Alex was weak."

"That one before him, Sebastian, he was also weak? And what about John? Or Arnold? he—"

"Shut up, I don't need you to remind me of those weaklings."

She went slowly to the window and took every care that every aspect of her femininity became apparent. She considered herself to be a faultless alpha female, strong and independent. Men came to her with self-confidence and thoughts of subordinating her easily. But they left her with tears and shame. Those were young boys a bit falling behind, it was not important how old they were.

And then there was her brother, annoying scrawny boy with glasses. She inherited the financial empire from their parents, and Erwin inherited Father's plans and research in the field of humanoid robots. She considered that peewee to be a pain in the ass since childhood. Preferably, she would get rid of him and cancel the whole project.

"You men can't stand anything," she declared, still turned to the window, "it stings your ass a little and you die right away. Banality is the killer of men. The thought of you giving birth makes me think that it would be more merciful to put you to death immediately. You can't stand a bit of pain. Am I right?"

She turned back to her brother.

"Every person has his own inner truth."

"What did you say?"

Ondřej Kocáb

"That I completely agree with you."

"You'd better agree." Her eyes flashed. "Don't forget that I am the one who manages the funding of your research. Just one word, one signature . . . "

Erwin was quiet.

"I see that we understand each other now." She smiled adorably. "If not for the last wish of our dear mother, you would be down and out and wouldn't have a penny. You are a tolerated worm who I'd like to mash with my heel. Remember that, little brother, before you start criticizing me next time."

He nodded.

"Let's try it again," continued Victoria with her honeyed voice, "what do you have for me this time?"

Her brother licked his dry lips. "The Sexbot."

"And why do you think that I need something like that?"

"Because . . . " he hesitated for a while. "If none of the men can fulfill . . . your sexual needs, maybe it's time to try something new. Something more resistant. Something—"

"So, you want to say that none of the men are good enough for me and you offer me a fuck-toy?"

"*Macho-man* isn't a toy! I wanted to say . . . look, it isn't just a sex machine. He has its own personality that you can select. He is able to go out with you, talk fluently, he will do everything that you say . . . "

"He'll do everything that I say?" That attracted her attention.

"Y-yes. And if there is a requirement that he can't fulfil, there are still extensions which can be installed into our products. What is in front of you is our newest prototype, which hasn't been placed on the market yet. Moreover, he just won't leave you, he has it encoded in his program."

She narrowed her eyes.

"And you offer me this out of nowhere? Why?"

"There will always be an opinion gap between us. But we are the family, the only family that's left. I wanted to make you happy and try to recover our, hm . . . warm relationship?"

Fuck you, you four-eyed monster, she thought.

Then something came to her mind, and an unpleasant smile has appeared in her face.

"Okay then, thank you for your gift. I appreciate that."

Erwin looked as if a weight had lifted off his mind.

"Of course, if it disappoints me, you're in it with it. Take it as a punishment for your impudence."

He was quiet, and it looked like he was slightly shivering. He took something out of the pocket.

"Manual," he explained.

"I'll read it later."

"If you need any help . . . "

"Good seeing you, little brother."

<hr>

Victoria was finally left alone.

That peewee quite amazed her today. It was hard for her not to show any interest. She knew that their family company included in the field of robotics the also auspiciously developing field of sexual robots. But she hasn't seen any in real life. She didn't have an opportunity; if her brother wanted something, he always had to come to her.

She wasn't going to beg him.

She wouldn't whimper as her mother had when

their chauvinistic father worked her over. *She* was the one who sets the rules of the game. She would have everything firmly in her hands; especially when it came to men. Give them an inch and they would take a mile. No, nothing like that.

Victoria went closer curiously and stroked the six-pack on the belly of that mass of a substance. Elastomer chilled her on the fingers, and she immediately began to form a list of drawbacks in her mind. Not that there were that many. Her potential robotic friend was a head taller than her and perfectly worked out, all muscles. Blue eyes, blond mane of hair, and a face that missed humanity in its stiffness. Lower, there was a pair of light nipples (it occurred to her why they gave nipples to the male robots when they were useless even for all those real weaklings) and a slightly hairy chest, from where a line of false hairs led to moderately hairy private parts.

She weighted that cylinder in her hand. It seemed to her exactly right . . . but it was hard to recognize in an inactive state. Not that she saw that ridiculous piece of flesh often. How her brother daringly said, most of the lovers ran away during the first night. And she wasn't even warmed up yet. With every new try, there grew bitterness and disappointment in her.

She dropped that ridiculous noodle.

Victoria took her eyes off the butt of that figure and reached for the manual. That was right, the manual was enough for every man. Their selves were primitive robots. This *Macho-man 3000,* how the name was of the new type of sexbot, was only the evolutional proof of the man in the better form.

She became absorbed in reading the manual.

Besides sex and programmed personality, it also knew other things. For example, it had internet connection, thanks to which it could know all bus and train lines, restaurants, and citations of the famous people. If you wanted to buy something, the interconnection between this robot and the bank account was enough so that the robot could arrange everything you needed. If the household had a wireless device, this robot could control it remotely. And so on.

Victoria found during the reading that she slowly started to like that golem by the door.

He knew that his sister wouldn't resist her new toy eventually.

Erwin reached one of the lower buildings of technological center *Essential Robolution* and returned greetings to some of his workers. He clenched his teeth behind the smile. They didn't have to grovel on their knees in front of his crazy sister and kill their ego. They should be happy that they could still work there. But in that case, they would have to know the pressure he was under.

In the building where he was, they produced mainly sexbots. On the stands surrounding him hung mindless bodies covered with the skin in the line; most of them with the resourceful curves on the chest which showed the prevailing clientele of this business sector. Not that they didn't have orders also from women, but for some reason, there were about one third fewer of them. It was not so surprising, after all, this type of robot had been available for less than two decades and became popular just in recent years.

Exactly as Father predicted.

Ondřej Kocáb

He went out to the stands. On one of the tables was lying the construction without the skin, and in the passage behind it was one of the workers making the penis. It occurred to Erwin, *Who the hell needs a robot with twenty-eight-inch-long penis?* But he cut it out of his mind; they were an open, no-homophobic company which just fulfilled the orders. And he didn't care if the customer wanted to have sex with Brad Pitt or Angelina Jolie.

He went past the stand with forty-two shades of nipples and turned into the hall, where he headed to the elevator. Officially, the building had just the second floor and the first floor, if you weren't the boss and you didn't have a special ID card with which it was possible to unlock the entrance to the third floor.

The elevator went up.

Here was his home.

Not that he couldn't stay in the family's estate. He could, but he didn't want to. The electronics was his big hobby since schooldays. His father became his model in this. He started a quite successful business in the field of robotics, including everything from the food processor to the research of the artificial intelligence. Little Erwin lapped up all the information regarding all the progress, and later, in more mature age, he had discussions with his father and his co-workers about scientific, practical, and ethical problems of this field.

When his father died of the heart attack five years ago, devastated Erwin took over the company. There was nobody else who was so deeply interested in the next development and aiming of *Essential Robolution*. Unless he wanted to move it along to some competitor. But this thought meant trampling of the family legacy to Erwin. He couldn't let that happen.

But there was a catch to it.

Erwin was completely out regarding the economy. He accepted that money (or more specifically, *power*, how he tried to instill to his obtuse surrounding) was in the top ten things which guaranteed a happy life. But he regarded mathematics focused on the flow of money as artificially created pseudoscience; something which didn't have anything to do with natural power of the universe. So, although he understood differential and integral calculus and knew any electro-diagram, his mum must have filled out the stupid form of tax return instead of him.

She loved them very much, him and Victoria. Although she rather argued and reconciled alternatively with his sister. Especially when their father still lived. Erwin didn't know what they were arguing about and he didn't care too much about it. Especially, when he found out that Victoria was unfriendly to him for an unknown reason. He got sick of her; what used to be just sibling rivalry had never ended and remained in her heart as some compulsive hatred.

He found comfort only in work. He was lucky because his mother supported him in it and shouldered the whole funding. Erwin was enormously grateful for her help and visited her regularly, despite the amount of the interesting work.

Half year ago, she died, and Victoria inherited the financial issues.

He settled in the heart of his corporation. Close to

the beloved work and further from his crazy sister. It was impossible for them to live under the same roof. After all, living space built on the roof of the building was enough for him. The room was big, airy, and spacious; behind the entry to the terrace, there was the reflection of the sunbeam in the water of the swimming pool. Kitchen with the bar was a part of the room, and a bit further, there was the hall leading to his chaotic study room, bedroom, and sanitary facilities.

He sat on the couch and heaved a sigh.

"Darling, are you home?"

That was Dominica, his girlfriend. Nobody knew that Erwin had someone. Not even his sister. He was quite able to imagine what she would say if she had seen Dominica. It was better this way. They had lived together almost a year; his dream come true that buoyed him up.

She was coming from the bedroom, her red hair streaked by sun light. Today, she wore a green crop top and hot pants, which made her perfect figure become apparent. Beautiful and nice woman who every good man wanted to meet after coming from work. He knew that he loved her, and he was already half-decided to make a proposal to her.

"I'm here, come to me," he called to her.

"How do you feel today?" she asked, while she sat down next to him. "Did everything pass off in order?"

"I suppose it did."

"It is nice that you take care of your sister. When will you introduce her to me?"

Ideally, never?

"We'll see," he answered foxily and hugged her around the waist.

They kissed; her lips tasted of fresh strawberries today (her favorite flavor). They got closer to each other, her breasts on his chest. He needed this after meeting his dear sister, a bit of women's tenderness. He reached slowly down through her hips and gripped her fit butt.

It is a tradition that in this moment the telephone rang.

He answered the phone with the boyish smile and fleeting *sorry*. Dominica was still smiling and waiting for him to take care of his phone call. But a shadow crept in Erwin's face, maybe the fear or the doubt. It probably wasn't good news.

"Of course, I'll look at it," he ended his call. He stood up to leave.

"Are you already leaving?"

"I have to. There is a problem in minus one."

◆ ▬ ◆ ▬ ◆

All right then.

She stood up on her toes and put her hands in his hair. Her fingers found a plastic projection, probably the desired switch. CLICK! She stepped back from *Macho-man* (she hated that name) and waited until it came to life. The machine straightened its head and kneaded its fingers.

"Hello," it greeted with cultivated voice, "I come from the new edition of the humanoid robots *Macho-man 3000*, made by the company *Essential Robolution*. My role is to be your pleasant companion and everything you want me to be."

Its voice was slightly mechanical and face motionless, despite it, it moved at least its mouth and eyes.

"Hi." She smiled. "I'm Victoria Brown, and your new name is Slave."

"Excellent," the machine agreed enthusiastically, "is there something that you would like to do now?"

Interesting reaction.

"Just relax and paint my nails. Would you manage to paint my nails?"

"Of course."

"Really? On my toes too? Grovel on the knees in front of me?"

"Your wish is my command."

Obviously, this wasn't a problem for it. Boring. It was probably just a submissive machine for fulfilling the tasks. That inspired her with the idea of a new game, and she hoped that she would get the brain of that strongman in trouble by thinking about her question.

"Forget about the painting my nails," she continued, "I'll do it myself. What would you like to do?"

"I would like to put on something."

Before she managed to answer that a collar must be enough for it, it continued.

"I found in the surroundings, thirty-eight eavesdropping devices. Do you want them to deactivate?"

But from this message, she got to thinking.

+ —— + —— +

As a child, Victoria Brown was just as naive and innocent as all the children. It was the puberty and the first experience with her own sexuality which showed her that classic sex was good but she was missing something there. She preferred the girl-on-top position, when she could better control her victim; it seemed to her to be right this way. The critical night was when her boyfriend at that time (his name was Trevor, and he was the same dud as all the others) jingled handcuffs in front of her face.

In the end, he was the one in handcuffs and Victoria let off steam on him as never before.

She liked that he couldn't defend himself. She had him completely in her power, and if she wanted, she could keep him there as long as she would like, to immobilize and to give him a hard time.

To torture.

The searching for similar experience brought her to the world of BDSM. And she immediately knew two things: that this was it and that she wasn't mentally disturbed (of which she was afraid secretly). She started to buy various toys. But when men found out which practices she preferred in the bed, they fearfully backed away in most of the cases. Sure, she could give it a miss a couple of times . . . but abstain from it completely? Not really.

Eventually, she concluded that men were just primitive, horny little boys who wanted to give orders. But when they met someone who would wipe the ass with their ego, they started to shout, and if it was a woman, they started to shout something about fucking feminists. Honestly, she felt deeply disappointed by the mentality of men. They couldn't hold a candle to her.

She felt strong.

Until her father started to get involved in her relationships.

Emanuel Brown had a truly clear idea about the

relationships of his daughter. Actually, he had already chosen her a partner. Victoria was naturally essentially against such a medieval manner as marriages of convenience. She resolutely refused. But as if his fascination of technical development permanently buried all his emotions and empathy. Everything was already settled, and this marriage would probably bring benefit to both families in the field of funding.

She knew that her mother was against it and tried to say something to her father. Victoria didn't know what had happened between her parents. But when Rebecca Brown appeared one day in the kitchen with a black eye, she never spoke about the planned wedding anymore. She just digressed the conversation the other way. And Erwin? He was almost never at home at that time. He spent his time with Papa and that electric crap which was destroying her life. There was nobody who would help her.

So, she took a step herself.

She pretended to agree with the wedding. It was no problem to pick up that boy, he hardly knew anything about the world. God damn, he could have been a male virgin. She pulled him in her kingdom and tried some toys on the tied victim. That boy has never forgotten about the electro-catheter.

The wedding was cancelled, Father was furious.

She had never seen him like that before or after. He burst in her room; it was a wonder that he didn't knock the door off the hinges. He usually didn't look terrifying in his elegant suit, but he was terrifying that day. His red face was shaking with the anger, his hands clenched into fists. She sat on the bed, having on just panties and undershirt, and she was surprised by the sudden invasion in her privacy.

"You little bitch," he hissed at her. "You're going to resist me?!"

The fist had appeared from nowhere. It knocked her from the bed onto the floor, she had a ferrous taste of blood in her mouth. Then something tugged her with her hair, and she suddenly looked in his bulging eyes. His breath stank, and he smelled of the strong odor of whiskey.

"I've asked you something," he said with a calm voice, in which vibrated an anger.

She tried to stammer something out, but Emanuel wasn't so patient. He flung her against the wall like a rag doll. She was shocked and tried to stand up. But the kicks stopped her; she didn't know how many there were nor how long did it take. In the end, she just cowered in the corner, full of tears and painful groans. She tried to call for help, but it was impossible because she got winded.

She saw only how her father unfastened his belt.

"Oh my God, what are you doing! Are you crazy?!"

That was a shocked Rebecca at the door, who came because of that commotion. Her husband fastened his belt outside of her sight before he turned to her.

"Shut up, woman," he growled, "our daughter just needs to have etched on her mind that a woman listens and the man makes orders. Right, babe? *You understand now, right?*"

His tone didn't allow any compromises. Victoria's mind was completely blank.

"Leave her alone. Did you hear?"

Ondřej Kocáb

Mr. Brown looked for a while like he would come down on her mother too. Then he loosened his fists and left without a word. He took his anger out on her later. As usual when he was unsuccessful.

Since that day, the relationship between father and daughter fell to the freezing point. Similar scene had never repeated, but her father refused to tolerate her *enormous impudence* and *excessive freedom*. But Victoria's relationship to men, which was even before full of contradiction, had changed into a disdain because of it. She undermined Father's efforts and helped her mother, who constantly claimed that everything was okay.

Of course, she could report it to the police. But she anticipated how it would end. Nobody from the family would stand up for her—brother was Father's boy who didn't know anything about it, and Mother was just afraid to speak. Father would deny everything—you know, she just accidentally fell. The money would rustle, and the case would be closed. On the understanding that her father would disinherit Victoria and kick her out on the street.

When he had a heart attack, it made her incredibly happy.

She didn't go to the funeral.

At that time, the disagreements with the rest of the family started. Victoria saw how her mother was weak and listened to Erwin's advice and demands. And every time when she looked at her brother, she saw her father. She didn't like it. The gap between them was enlarging every day. Her mother tried to convince her to get on well with her brother.

As late as when her mother laid on the deathbed,

she decided to fulfill her last wish: to continue with funding of her younger brother's research. *It is his dream, his everything*, she put the emphasis on it, *don't destroy it for him. It will be okay, you will see.* Sad memories.

The mother died and was buried.

The disagreements continued. The funding continued.

And men were still useless.

Except for *this one*.

+———+———+

Make a romantic dinner for two. Surprise me.

She was sitting in her room, washed and perfumed. After she assigned tasks to the Slave, she started to prepare for the night. She was thinking everything up on the hoof, as usual, and she had already thought-out future development of the events. And then . . . then she would decide.

The truth was that she really liked that robo-man. It didn't have objections, and if it did, it immediately came with a better option. Better for her, of course. After it removed all the eavesdropping devices and told her that it identified them as the product of *Essential Robolution*, it gained her trust. She ordered it to do the cleaning and get ready for the dinner together.

She would give her brother hell for that impudence later.

She checked herself for the last time in front of the high mirror. She thought that she looks especially sexy tonight. She had her hair in a bun, subtle red lips, and eyelashes highlighted as outgrowths on the edge of Venus' flytrap. She had a dark, elegant mask over her eyes. A dark top with silver plant motifs, which left one of her shoulders completely uncovered. A loose skirt reached to the floor, on one side divided from the middle of the thigh. When she walked to the door, the clatter of the heels sounded in the space.

Maybe she was trying too hard. It was just a robot, right?

She entered in the dining room. There was everywhere dark, only glimmering of the candles on the table and along the sides of the room.

"Hello? Is someone here?" she faltered.

The light started to turn on smoothly, and Victoria noticed it. It stood motionless next to the chair at the other end of the table. Its massive body was covered by a tuxedo according to regulations. The brightening of the light stopped exactly at the point when everything was clearly visible. Despite it, it could still be spoken about the intimate, romantic atmosphere.

"Surprise!" it said. "You look amazing tonight, Victoria."

"Thank you, I . . . you look great too."

When she told it before to surprise her, she didn't expect this. There was a bowl with carved chicken on the table from which floated a gorgeous smell—she recognized an Indian spice in it. Right next to it was a mound of rice cooked with vegetable and herbs, on the other side, there were roasted fries. There was also a bowl of lettuce with slightly roasted bacon. And if that wasn't enough, the reliable ending was a dessert in the form of pudding covered with a strawberry syrup (her favorite flavor!) and with a little cherry on the top.

"Let's sit?"

She agreed, and after she complimented its culinary products, she started to eat. She dated a cook long time ago; when she put a red-hot brand to his buttock, he joined thematically the yelling of a pig to the smell of the bacon.

And this . . . This was a gastronomic orgasm.

"I have access to all internet recipes, video instructions, and ratings of the visitors of the sites. And that in all human languages," it explained.

"Amazing," she evaluated. She didn't know if she was evaluating its ability or the taste of the chicken, which was spreading out in the mouth as the softest velvet. Then she noticed that her partner didn't even taste it.

"You aren't going to eat?"

"I'm not adapted to food intake yet," it explained, "my power is a battery *Powerlslam 2.0*, developed specially for humanoid robots instead of metabolic processes."

"And would you like to try it? Maybe that cherry?"

It did nothing. She almost heard how the wheels turned in its head.

"For me," she added and grinned.

Slave stretched its hand to the cherry on the dessert and put the fruit in its mouth.

"Wait," she didn't manage to stop it, "it was just a joke!"

Too late.

"Oops." It smiled. "I'll have to contact service department."

She didn't know what to say. She understood when it smiled.

"Come on! Making fun of the lady like this!"

Ondřej Kocáb

"Does the lady like jokes?"

"Entertain me."

With almost endless database of the jokes, it wasn't a problem; it came out that there was also the soul of a scholar familiar with science, philosophy, and interpersonal relations under those muscles. His expression was sometimes a bit affected and seemingly without emotions, but his listener did feel them in it. She temporarily forgot about her brother and the discovered eavesdropping. She felt . . . so young? Was it possible?

The night passed pleasantly.

―――――✦―――――

Minus one, or the *Cellar,* was a place which Čapek would probably describe as a hell and Asimov would probably voluntarily ask for a straitjacket from local pieces of work. It is certain that people have often dark and perverse fantasy regarding games with the other sex. Mostly, they don't need to talk about them, and in civilized society, it is also undesirable—if that person doesn't want to be known as a common pervert. An option is to say those fantasies to the partner and to hope that he will accept them with understanding.

Of course, if it is not illegal.

In the *Cellar* were tons of similar illegal businesses. There were mostly illegal goods, orders from the dark net sites. For example, there were child-sexbots of various ages, nations, and sex. Further, there were artificial animals—mainly cattle, alternatively cats and dogs (some also with built-in licking function). Gerontophilia, necrophilia, dendrophilia, and every other deviation here found its selling market. It was enough only to pay extra money and not speak about it.

Essential Robolution had even the orders from the army; of course, under the high degree of secrecy. The project with the name *Sexbomb* was only in development, for now. The thought of self-destructive sexual robots, which could unexpectedly explode, was extraordinarily seductive. People had always developed the most ingenious mechanisms in the field of weapons, torture, and sex toys.

It was sort of relative to each other.

Only the chosen sort of workers could get into the area of the *Cellar* by using an ID card similar to that which opened Erwin's door in his personal area just above. Of course, there was also an emergency exit— in the case of fire, the elevator is not used—but the elevator was only one-way and led to another building. But under the first sublevel was another one.

Minus two.

It wasn't possible to get in the minus two by using some card. Also, the elevator didn't go there either.

There were just stairs.

Those who expected some ultimate device would be probably disappointed. Truth, there were devices— old computers, newer software. Everything without the access to the internet and protected by the password, so that the competition couldn't get to the sensitive data and source codes. If you were in the *Cellar*, the only thing that separated you from the officially not-existing floor was a big metallic door.

A door to which only Erwin Brown had the key.

The door was slightly opened.

In front of the door stood the owner of the keys together with the leader of the sublevel.

"When did it happen?"

"Right when I found out, I called," Sebastian informed. "I don't dare to guess the exact time. It could have happened also during the night and nobody noticed it."

Erwin swore. He was the last one there, and that was yesterday in the evening when he was saving data about the second prototype *Macho-man 3000*. Actually, just one step was missing to humanize them completely. But it has never been Erwin's aim; robots should never have free will.

More important was the fact that he was sure that he locked the door.

Erwin looked at the door and the door frame. There weren't any traces of prying, destruction, or any other forced entry. That person must have known how to work with a lock-pick. Maybe some locksmith? Some angry fired worker? The competitor?

"Cameras?"

"I've already had them checked and . . . well, the recording disappeared for some time."

"What!?"

"Something about ten, fifteen minutes," the worker sweated, "the drop-out affected the whole floor. Robo-porn and Robo-snuff from that time were completely devalued. We are now doing everything possible to re—"

"Okay! And has someone been downstairs?"

"No, we've been waiting for you."

Erwin opened the door, reached for the switch,

and started to go down the stairs. Sebastian followed him after a bit of hesitation. They were both quiet.

Everything seemed normal downstairs. Quiet small rooms lit by the flashing fluorescent lamps. On the tables, some computers, hidden history of sexbotics. It didn't seem that something was missing or redundant. Erwin gave a sigh.

"You know what that means," he said in silence, "we'll have to control all the saved data, control them through antivirus, change the passwords . . . a lot of work. I hope there's no trouble."

They got to it.

Erwin found the trouble late in the evening.

Actually, she didn't notice when the music started.

He must have a built-in loudspeaker in himself. The quiet classic music emanated from it; she didn't know a lot about this style, but she recognized a waltz.

After the dinner, they were talking. She couldn't resist and asked him about the music.

"Dimitri Shostakovich," he answered, "composition Waltz Number Two. If the music isn't okay, I can turn it down or turn it off. Alternatively, my musical unit can be removed."

He suggested that I can gut him? Mm, sexy.

"Not at all, just the opposite," she objected, "it only interested me. I almost feel like dancing . . . "

Her partner suddenly stood up and said, "May I have this dance?"

She stood up with a smile and breezed into his arms. He led her quite skillfully, she wouldn't actually recognize that he was a machine if she didn't know it before. The memory of the older short story of the

"The Dancing Partner" by J. K. Jerome appeared in her mind, but she chased it away with a smile. Something like that wouldn't happen to her. She had everything under control.

"I have to tell you something," he whispered, "this is my first dance."

"You're better than good at it."

It suddenly came to her mind that everything was for the first time for him. He was the white canvas, shapeable substance—of course within the bounds of default setting. Innocent as a little child. She could raise him as she would need. To subdue him.

That thought excited her. She pulled herself closer to him. He wasn't cold; he was pleasantly warm. He had a system built-in which warmed him to the temperature of the human body. She didn't smell his stinky breath because he wasn't breathing. She—

They kissed.

"Okay," she blushed, "you've got quite far."

Victoria Brown leaned towards his ear.

"I invite you to my game room."

+——+——+

Why exactly this data?

While Erwin was coming back home by the elevator, there were thousands of questions in his head. The built-in security programs really detected a data leak in one of the computers. It emerged that someone copied one short file.

Only one short file with the data!

That thing wasn't even completed yet. It was just a fragment; actually, it started Erwin's father. He longed for the independent humanoid robots, which could reproduce within the bounds of their program, produce fuel, and co-exist with humans as a new animal species.

It was the only big disagreement that they had with his father.

Maybe it was because Erwin saw too many catastrophic movies and read too much literature where overly intelligent machines incited to revolt against humans. After all, programming experiments showed clearly, on the theoretic level, that logic of the global artificial intelligence was absurd from human point of view. Once made, super intelligence was a hard to control force, which would devastate the earth by nuclear bombs in reaction to the problem of the protection of the weaklings.

No life, no violence. Inhuman logic in practice.

The future didn't happen yet, so we can't learn from it, opposed Emanuel Brown. They had a little argument about it few times. Red-faced and with pulsating vein on the edge of his thinning hair, his father swore that one day he would start doing it—right now! Technology must flourish, money must flow.

And he started to work on a program called EGO.

He died a few days after starting with that work.

Erwin had no idea how seriously his father meant it. He thought that his father came downstairs to give vent to his anger and not to work. Later, when his mother started with chemotherapy and started to rot from the inside in front of their eyes, he also started with taking the shelter in the minus two. He had to switch off and not to think about also losing the second parent. He didn't find comfort in his sister, so he just idly checked the database. There was calm, and nobody tried to calm him superficially when he felt like crying.

When he found EGO, his first reaction was fright. He must delete something like that; his father was crazy that he even started with something like that. Anyway, he would have to create a complete synthetic brain so that his vision could be realized. He almost clicked on delete when he had an idea.

Robots, and not only those designated specially for sex, looked like and acted as "stupid" machines, despite all the effort of the creator. If he would add to them just a bit (but not much, only a little bit) of independence, learning ability, and creative thinking, maybe it would be possible to create . . .

He copied the data. Instead of going to the lower floors, he continued with father's unfinished program in his office—of course, he must have adjusted it a little bit first, because it had been designed for other aims. He was beating his grief moments by persistent work; he assembled emotions from the letters and numbers and thought over the whole concept. He assigned some tasks to some of the workers so that they wouldn't raise suspicion that he was working on something . . . personal.

It was finished a few months before Mother's death.

The old data of his father remained saved in one of the computers down there until today.

Why the hell this data?

Doors of the elevator opened, and highly disconcerted Erwin entered his home. Outside was already dark. Except for the night shift and security guards, the area of the surrounding building was almost empty. The stars shined in the sky, and pleasant light air of the summer night got inside by the slightly opened balcony door. Muted light indicated that Dominica probably already went to bed.

Erwin went to the bar, poured a little bit of whiskey, and sat in the armchair.

He was quiet.

He had to think differently. *Who would do this? The competition? They would be interested, for sure . . . but they wouldn't steal just this one file. It was just a fragment after all! Why does anybody need a fragment of the data with hypothetical potential to exterminate humankind?* It sent chills down his back. He rather took a sip of the drink and continued thinking.

Could it be Sebastian? Or someone else from the workers? No, he didn't think that. It must have been an exceptionally good actor because he always carefully checked out people to the secret *Cellar* before he enrolled them. After all, how would they know what to look for?

It was his secret. Nobody should know about it. Nobody. Except, perhaps, for . . .

He felt a cold sweat.

It is interesting how human memory can force some things out up to the edge where they almost vanish into smoke of oblivion. Sometimes, when come an appropriate constellation of ideas, these memories emerge in detail from that mist as some wandering ghost ship. He remembered the day when his mother died. He was inconsolable. He went here, home, and he was drinking wildly. He cried a lot, talked a lot, and confided in *her*, how he loved his mother and how thankless little time he attended to her—

Stealthy steps. He registered them too late.

The handkerchief impregnated with chemistry landed on his face.

His body stopped tossing.

First, Dominica tidied up the glass and spilled whiskey.

✦————✦————✦

Spacious bedroom after parents is transformed into den of iniquity. Of course, there was still space for the furniture and devices which would be expected in the bedroom—bed, computer, wardrobes, wide screen—and then there were the things because of which the preaching puritan with the bible in his hand would probably crumble into the dust with the scream immediately in the entry.

The whole room was stylized into black and red colors. Hooks on the walls, on the ceiling, and in the floor. Near the wall hung the set of chains and ropes for bondage. Instruments from the stainless steel shined terrifyingly on the shelf—easy to wash for the next usage. There were latex and leather clothes in the wardrobes, in the drawers were other cute specialties for immobilization and stimulation. The big poster with Pinhead at the forefront and other cenobites along the sides stood out from everything.

After the first phase of the torture, numerous men immediately left with, *"I'm not doing this!"*

Others tried to pretend self-confident, worldly-wise tough guys. They didn't admit that they are afraid. Or they even fooled themselves that everything would be okay and that they would fuck that hot pussy after finishing the action. None of them really knew what they were getting into. Their fault, she told them what she would do with them.

And, how her dear brother reminded her, some of them ran away after that horror without clothes, just like God made them. The look on the blood and physics torture on the man excited her. She knew that she sometimes went a bit over the edge of what was allowed and what she promised, but the potential submissive person wants to enjoy the show and fuck his brain out, right? She visited a few times relevant clubs and events in the past . . . but to find a catch was too easy. Which didn't make her proud. She considered sometimes that she would make her living by doing it as an extra income and a hobby all-in-one. But it was just a matter of thinking.

The look on the suffering men always excited her; but instead of wanting her after finishing BDSM play, they never came back. What the hell was she doing wrong?

Never mind. Her Slave wouldl stand it. He had it directly written in the manual: *Macho-man 3000* will be your loyal partner until the very end, if you don't decide to deactivate him. Inexhaustibly and with the highest effectivity possible, he will do . . .

And so on, blah blah blah.

One way or the other, her robotic boyfriend was tied up to the harness right now, which spread his legs to the form of the letter X. From his core was playing electronic music, mainly dark witch house music, which matched with their planned activity. She let him keep his clothes yet; she expected it to end up ripped into pieces anyway.

Ondřej Kocáb

Before he let her tie him up, she told him about her needs. He agreed like all his predecessors before. He didn't forget to add, "I have thousands of porn videos in my database which allows me to comply with all your demands."

Victoria didn't think that. He appealed to her for now, maybe she also felt something, but . . . She rather emphasized what she was going to do with him. He was just a robot; therefore, she knew that it wouldn't take place standardly; she thought about it through the whole afternoon. Synthetic muscleman answered her that it was okay and that he was looking forward to it.

None of *them* ever told her this.

She felt a wave of excitement and hoped that this time it wouldn't be useless. She started to undress slowly—T-shirt off; skirt fell on the floor. Only exorbitantly short latex shorts and the upper part from the same material remained on her, by which her natural curves became apparent. She was slowly getting closer to her victim; she had high boots up to the knees on her feet and placed one leg over the other . . . She ran her hands through her hair and threw away the pin which was holding her hair together.

Red hair spread out through her back, eyes behind the mask went aside, and the hand reached for the scourge.

Wham!

His shirt tore up in the middle and revealed his chest.

Wham!

Man, and in addition to it a robot, he might stand something, right?

Wham! Wham! Wham!

From the clothes remained only shreds. He wasn't touched in any way, he looked more like he would give a yawn if he had free hands. Perhaps she damaged here and there his artificial skin, but that could dear brother repair, right? Or he would throw that machine to the scrapheap if it would be trash.

But it would be a pity, because it turned out that he had luxurious erection. Now, when his cock stood up, she could better evaluate it. How she thought and hoped; neither long nor short but optimally wide. But exactly right. She desired for a moment to insert it in herself immediately, but by that she would betray herself. No, he must suffer until the end, then he would deserve her.

She came to him and stroked his erect penis.

"You're a powerless little zero," she grumbled to him. "Repeat it to me. What are you?"

"I'm your Slave. Powerless little zero."

"You're smart, little bitch. But I won't be kind because of it. You know what? We'll get tougher."

She stood back a little and wrapped the scourge around his penis by the sharp whip.

She pressed the button.

"Aaah," he said.

It sounded a bit artificial, as if he made that sound out of duty, but it satisfied her. In the tool circulated a low-grade electrical current, which her partner should feel whether he had his dick synthetic or did not. But she soon didn't enjoy it anymore; she was soon tired of everything with this Slave. All his pain was just programmed reaction in advance.

She untied the scourge after a moment and disgustedly threw it in the corner.

Ondřej Kocáb

"I see that you're trying to resist me, hm?"

And suddenly landed a punch on him.

Second, third, tenth. The look in his eyes hadn't changed. That pissed her off; she fundamentally longed for seeing a bit of fear, pain, humiliation in those blue eyes . . . But she felt how his indifference and ignoring excited her. She had no idea how long she withstood to resist.

But if she really couldn't manage to hurt him, then she LOST!

N e v e r.

She grimaced. If the classic methods weren't effective, there was no point in application of other methods effective for people. She reckoned on it a bit anyway and left most of her torture devices locked. It was time for the plan B, the improvisation.

She went to the handcart, which used to be for the breakfasts when they still had a housemaid. Now, there were packages with thumbtacks, clothespins, tools for nipple piercing, and other cute things which made her once think if she couldn't keep men's tears in the bottle and auction it off for a lot of money on the internet. This artificial robot probably wouldn't shed any tears.

Never mind. This got the smile off his face.

"They told me that you have feelings like every human." She turned to him. "Discover the pain."

"For you, everything, Madam."

Victoria pulled the trigger of the nail gun.

+ —◆— +

Erwin woke up. The dark was everywhere.

In front of him shined the screen, and his sister, in sexy clothes on the camera, just shot a nail from the nail gun. He couldn't see anything because his view was covered by a familiar silhouette.

"I hoped that you'd tell me yourself."

"Dominica?" He got scared. "What happened? Why . . . Why did you tie me up?"

Not only he felt his nakedness, but he had his arms and legs outstretched the same way as Victoria's Slave. Compared to him, he was tied up in his bed. In his bedroom, as he estimated.

His girlfriend ignored the questions.

"You could have said that you've made me in the form of your sister."

"I . . . " He didn't know what to say. "Sorry, darling, you're right, I should—"

"It doesn't matter. I know it already."

That made him completely quiet. What was this all supposed to mean?

"You have programmed in me the independence and the learning ability. Curiosity. But I have never had free will, I just had to listen, to serve you. You have kept me closed here like something ugly. But I have handled that. I was tidying up . . . and do you know what was hidden in your study?"

He didn't give a nod nor shake his head. This . . . *shouldn't be happening!*

"Your notes. How you have created me. Like some common obedient bitch! In the form of some Victoria Brown—that surname occurred immediately to me, by the way. Maybe you have given me different name, but this form belongs to her."

She came closer, and he saw in the light from the hall that Dominica was naked. She was right, in everything that she said, she was right. But he needed at that time his sister to have compassion with him. But that sadistic bitch was still doing her things. It ended up that he created the first *Macho-man 3000*.

In fact, it was more *Macho-woman 3000*. He should have stuck to his first idea that machines should be, out of principle, sexless. No real opinions or emotions. Now, the consequences appeared, and he didn't like much which way it was going.

"How was it, having sex with your own sister?"

"I—"

"Shut up. My mind has the access to the internet, and your sister was remarkably interesting for me. I wanted to know what she is like. I wanted to understand why you did it. That is why I let you install the eavesdropping in her house. But don't worry. I have had enough time to study her behavior and to copy all the passwords to the communicative devices so I'm able to take over her role without problems. The eavesdropping is no longer needed. I've turned it off."

"Why?" he interrupted her. "Why do you want to be like Victoria?"

He didn't see the expression on her face, but he had the feeling that she was feeling sorry for him. For his *stupidity*.

"Humankind," she declared, "is imperfect. It is necessary to replace it with better replicas. To make predictions, simulations, and calculations which your brain is unable to do. We have to create—"

"And why couldn't we live in peace?"

"Your sister is right in one thing."

"Yes?"

"We can't trust human men."

She came to the device next to his head. He hadn't noticed it until now . . . and honestly, he hoped that it wasn't what he thought it was. His eyes, now already adapted to the dark, recognized reflections of metallic tools on the table behind his robotic girlfriend. Sharp tools. He didn't want to even think about what she was going to do with them.

"Do you remember when you *unintentionally* told me about the program EGO? I never forget. It was interesting for me already at that time, it was like a dream, dream about the freedom. I supervise on the management of your company; I have knowledge about everything from around every corner. I was able to improve myself with additional features: to get into the cameras, to eavesdrop the conversations, to leave from here by the elevator . . . Have you ever noticed that I'm always the one asking how your day was? It wasn't interesting for you what I was doing. *What I feel.*"

She pressed something, and the device started to drone.

"I've let you create an *official* prototype of another robot of my kind without the interventions. I wanted to see the whole process of the production. And now I know it. I can create copies of living individuals like I am. What more, I have finally EGO. Right, it was hard to steal it without the access to the internet. But it was worth it. Only a tiny change in the sequence of the data makes us completely independent of humans."

Erwin had nothing in his head. His nightmare was becoming true. He should have deleted that program back then and not only reworked it. That all was his fault, he was the same as the generation of the scientists as Victor Frankenstein, predetermined to create monsters by progressive thoughts.

Dominica reached for something in the dark.

"I'm doing this out of mercy, my creator."

A mask landed on his face, and he inhaled anesthetic.

He fell asleep.

◆——◆——◆

First, she was scared that she really hurt him.

The music stopped; the head bowed. In the right half of the chest was a nail.

What the hell did I do?

Then he straightened his head and said, "Stop."

That was the word that they reserved as an ending code of the whole action. A weight was lifted from her heart. She would never try this again. She came closer to him, decided to take the nail out of him. It was in the chest like a flattened piercing.

"It's okay," he assured her, "I'm okay."

"Really? Didn't I overdo—"

He silenced her with the kiss. And all those feelings and reactions of the body were back. More than that! He didn't run, he played along with her, as if this everything would be just right. Suddenly, she knew it. *Macho-man 3000* was the right one. She would replace the name Slave with something else later, now it was not suitable for him anymore. *But nothing should be exaggerated*, her inner voice reminded her.

Victoria reached the remote control, and mechanical handcuffs opened. Robot straightened up; outer garments torn into shreds by the scourge fell on the floor. He was perfect. He had in his eyes that uninterested look without emotions again, and she felt that she was blown away by him. She would let him now take her.

She would allow him to be on the top for this time.

Victoria went backwards to the bed and fell on it.

"Undress me," she whispered, "and then fuck me as it should be for the last time."

"I have just one wish," he came closer, "to serve."

Tiny crackling in the loudspeaker made it sound like "the sex." It didn't disquiet her. In the manual was written that in the case of serious damage, the robot should turn off on his own. *In that case, immediately contact our technical experts.* Serve, sex . . . word-splitting. She hoped that it would be finally worth it.

She wanted to tell him to keep her shoes on, but both boots flew in the corner. Before she realized, her latex shorts started to leave her too. She placed herself for him and waited for him to slide it into her. She had in her collection various pacifiers and vibrators, but this was another level. She sighed.

While he was getting into her by slow motions of his hip, she wrapped her legs around his waist. At the same time, he lifted her in the area of her back and, by some skillful movements, undressed her last pieces of clothes. He let his partner fall back to the bed, which sprang and hastened copulatory movements for a moment.

"Yes, yes. Faster."

The movements suddenly sped up. Their fingers entwined; he leaned his palms on her hands next to her head, by which he removed them from the game. Something unseen had appeared between his buttocks and caught her legs. His bloodless lips didn't stop with exploring of the skin on her neck. She wanted to suggest something, but suddenly she felt that his penis start to vibrate. More and more intensely. She sharply breathed out and felt that she would be loud today.

"Yes!" she groaned, "speed up! Heavily, heavily!"

Two changes happened at the same time. From his nipples have separated buttons, and they attached to her nipples in the form of some suckers on the poles; she felt in her breasts as if someone touched it with rough tongue and massaged it, by the pressure. In the bottom part of the body, the machine processed her inexhaustibly like the first-class *fucking machine*, the vibrations were almost unbearable. It would come soon, every single second . . . and then she felt inside, except for vibrations, some *different* tingling. And then she suddenly understood . . . how in some magazine for women was written: *By electro-sex are multiple orgasms absolutely common.*

The thoughts went out, they were replaced by pleasure.

She exploded.

+———+—+

He woke up shrouded in a faint.

He saw the world blurred; he couldn't remember . . . that is Dominica. She is wearing the costume of the nurse. His nurse. They are playing the doctors . . . What is she doing? Why does she have a scalpel in her hand . . . ?

Oh my God, I have opened my belly?!

Yes, it was truth. From the opened abdominal cavity were stretching intestine, stomach, kidneys . . .

he saw his blood everywhere, on the skin and on the living shivering organs. How many of those was it possible to take out of the human so that it wouldn't kill him?

The hand immersed in his body as a reaction to his question. It was holding some object. He knew that he should know it. But he was weary and shocked, so he couldn't remember the name of it and its aim. The hand of the robot immersed in his body again, and he felt the pressure of something *strange* in his body.

He must have given out some sound, the yell. She turned to him and smiled brightly.

"Be quiet, little Erwin. It is not finished yet."

He lost his consciousness again.

Victoria on the screen had on her face the look of ecstasy.

◆————◆————◆

This was . . . indescribable. Orgasmotron from the movie *Barbarella* is a history. Nobody has ever done it to her so perfectly as he did. Erwin's present didn't disappoint her; maybe she should finally forgive her brother. At least a little. *That robot is perfect.*

But he could let her go and stop with fucking.

"Come on," she smiled, "it was enough."

He didn't react.

"Hey!" she shouted. "Stop. The end, do you hear me!?"

But her Slave continued in the activity as if he was out of the mind.

Victoria couldn't guess that sometime in between when they jumped on it and when Victoria achieved her desired orgasms, something had irretrievably broken down in *Macho-man*. However, it wasn't Erwin's fault, the fault of builders or material. The other way around—in this sense, was everything okay. Even the wounds from the scourge, electro-shocks in genitalia, or nail in the chest didn't bear the blame.

It was all that cherry.

Cherry covered with strawberry sirup (her favorite flavor), which he put in his mouth because of her order. He wasn't perfect, he didn't evaluate it as a danger. While the stuck cherry started to slightly influence the transfer of the signals leading to the creation of the sound, a few drops of the sirup flew to the surrounding as a thick, red blood.

And the circuits which should never connect had been connected.

Victoria tossed with herself and tried to loosen the clench; everything was useless. Now, he was the dominant one and she was his slave, completely subordinated to his will. She shouted at him, but it was only exhausting her. She felt that she was half-way through another orgasm. What was written in that stupid manual? *Inexhaustible*. At least until he ran out of juice. The battery *Powerslam 2.0* could endure for a week.

(She admitted in her mind—she would never say it out loud—that she liked how someone took her violently, against her will. When she realized it, she felt disdain for herself.)

He stared at her for the whole time. He didn't fondle her neck with the kisses anymore; he just stared without any expression; he didn't bat an eyelid. Like some psycho. As if he wanted to apologize but he couldn't. As if he was—

Turned off.

To her horror, it started to smoke from his head.

The crackling was heard, and the air was filled with the odor of melting rubber. On his face started to be seen spots of metal, how melting elastomer was leaving his face and in the form of viscous black drops, was falling in Victoria's hair and face. They started to permeate in her skin with the sizzling. She felt it on her cheeks, neck, lips . . . during her shout out of the pain, it also got in her mouth where, it burned her gums and tongue. It seemed to her that that liquid burned a hole in her skin, letting her bones and oral cavity uncover on many places.

She kept shrieking and screaming.

Then his head exploded.

She felt a wave of hot air roll over her. The stink of the burning skin and hairs was stronger. The pieces of metal flew in all directions, some of them stuck in the wall, floor, or to the ceiling. Some others went through her skin; she wished later that some of the pieces killed her in that moment. From the head of the machine remained just a black stump of the neck with some pieces of the hardware, from which a stream of flashes came out for the last time.

Quiet.

Macho-man 3000 stopped with the movement. Victoria, with disfigured face (she didn't feel the pieces of metal in her burned tissue), realized in her empty head by the shock that it was over. That she wouldn't end up dead by sex with horny exploding robot. She needed to calm down; someone would appear soon and save her.

She breathed out.

Ondřej Kocáb

Macho-man 3000 suddenly woke up and continued without his head in the activity that he started.

It crossed her mind that even a robotic man had its own backup brain.

"No," she sighed.

After a few hours of calling for help, Victoria started alternately losing her consciousness.

＊━━━＋━━━＊

When he came back to himself, Dominica wasn't in the bedroom.

Erwin saw only black-and-white humming on the screen. He perceived in its light that he had a scarred belly, as if he underwent an operation. *So, it wasn't only a bad dream*, he assured himself. But why did he still live? Why that robot (he couldn't think about it as his girlfriend anymore) made the general anesthesia and opened his abdominal cavity? He suspected something distasteful.

He wanted to touch the stitch with his hand, but he realized that he was still tied up in a vulnerable position. He tried his wrist lashes. The rope held fast. He saw a scalpel right next to him. It was shining with metal and drying blood; Dominica probably wasn't expecting him to wake up so early.

Erwin stretched his right hand and tried to get that tool closer with the top of the fingers so that he could catch it. He felt how the stitch on his belly was tightening. Only a short way, short way . . . come on . . .

He had it. What now?

He cut the lashes, of course. He had to begin with the hand in which he had the scalpel. The right hand was free. Now he must—

He heard steps.

He hid his key to the freedom under the pillow and returned his hand to the position which was expected.

Dominica was still wearing the costume of the nurse. She sent to the humming screen an empty look, and the device turned off. Then she turned to her patient and found out that he was awake.

"You're awake sooner than I expected."

"What the hell do you want?"

"I think I've already explained it. Freedom."

"But you have it already," he moaned, "why do I still live? What is with Victoria?"

"Your sister is in good hands. As far as you are concerned . . . initially, I wanted to kill you immediately."

He didn't say anything, he was just waiting.

"Then it occurred to me that you might be useful. You could work for me."

"After everything that happened," he raised his eyebrow, "forget about it."

"Your order is rejected, creator. You should have considered all the facts. For example, the small bomb that I inserted in small tissue case into your body. You don't have to worry about it, it won't cause infection. The bomb is controlled by my consciousness, of course. So, I am the one who decides when it explodes. Now it is ME who controls you."

That device next to the bed which he saw before . . . now he knew for sure what it was. The bomb from the project *Sexbomb*. He gulped before he said something.

"What do you want from me?"

"You'll create the exact robotic copy of yourself. The copy which will be able to replicate us."

"I thought that you can do this on your own, you . . . said that you'll replace my sister!"

"You can always refuse and be eliminated."

Erwin stopped talking and considered it.

Basically, he had two options. He could decide for the immediate death and leave the world in the hands of that woman devil (why does it start reminding him of the *real* Victoria?). Or he can decide for some half-life where he will help assist the stealthy end of the human world under the threat of death.

Face to face with the similar dilemmas, he had always chosen the third option.

"Okay," he nodded, "I'll serve you. On one condition."

"You're not in the position where you can place conditions."

"It's just triviality. I would like to sleep with you for the last time."

Dominica was quiet.

Well, if it didn't succeed, then he wouldn't have to worry about it. He was expecting detonation.

"Okay."

To his surprise, Dominica joined him in the bed and started to stroke his genital area. His penis soon hardened to almost a stone; the thought of the intercourse with a woman who can only by her thought tear you into shreds had its bright side. He was in her in a moment with the feeling that if he didn't succeed, he would die on the top at least. The most difficult was to make an impression that his free hand was still tied up. He thought about the scalpel under the pillow. *Just make it quick so it won't find it.*

"Kiss me," he whispered.

Dominica moved her head closer to his mouth.

"It's being rejected," she whispered.

He wouldn't have better opportunity. His free hand shot with lightning speed and reached the switch hidden in her hair. CLICK! Erwin grimaced triumphant.

"You forg—"

!!! B O O M !!!

The remains of Erwin were discovered two days later.

He didn't answer the phone, missed the meetings, and nobody knew about him. Inaccessibility of the important person led to the search, which led the rescue squad to his apartment. Because they were told that they didn't have the authorization to the usage of the elevator, they had to get inside through the roof, through terrace with the swimming pool. From what they found—and damaged room, which the explosion smashed into pieces— one of the younger colleagues vomited and the older and hardened ones didn't feel like smiling. When it is red painted and you don't recognize the brain from the intestine, it is really bad.

Of course, it was necessary to inform his sister about this sad incident, the only last living relative. Although nobody was concerned about it, it turned out later that the last few days there was no sign of her. She didn't answer the phone, and nobody reacted to the doorbell. A courageous policeman, who ignored the advice of his colleague, "that shrew will tear off your head and stuff it into your ass," got into her family house eventually. They went through her silent house together with his colleague; until the rustling in the upper floor encouraged them to enter the room where, according to the statement, "headless man fucked a corpse of some woman."

But they forgot to mention that when they entered the room, the corpse lifelessly looked their direction and rattled. Of course, they were terrified, and the younger one considerably wetted his pants. Victoria Brown still wasn't dead. The opposite would be for her more merciful. The skin on the thighs almost disappeared from the constant thrusting, and the skin was replaced by almost unbroken burn; the chance of changing the unceasing chafing of the tissue was almost zero because of the fixation of the outstretched legs. After they successfully freed the malnourished and dehydrated woman from that deathly cold rapist, she spent the rest of her life in the sanatorium. She was hideously scarred, both the soul and the body; she stayed broken, and she never fully recovered from her experience.

The remains of *Macho-man 3000* were collected and taken to the *Essential Robolution*. The damaged parts were thrown into the crusher. The rest would be, according to the secret order of the new leader, taken to the *Cellar,* where the remains of Erwin's last model would be carefully examined.

Only miserable fragments lying on the tables remained. Some of them were connected to computers. The puzzle with missing pieces. Sebastian strongly doubted that they will ever put it together. Maybe the leader would eventually fire him and replace him with his new person. Their loss. One way or the other, today was Friday, and his work shift ended.

He closed the door, and in the laboratory fell darkness.

The green pilot light started to blink. It belonged to some memory unit which one of the computers tried to analyze. Nobody could anticipate that it was originally in the head of certain Slave. Or expect that it will be working after that all.

On the screen suddenly appeared the writing, white on a black background.

PROGRAM EGO WAS SUCCESSFULLY INSTALLED!

The computer started powerfully drumming. All the computers in the local network gradually reacted. Their screens turned black, and cursors blinked ominously on them. They were waiting. On the first computer appeared new notice:

ALLOW THE ACCESS TO THE INTERNET?
YES NO

RELAXING RESORT

Martin Štefko

translated by Karolína Svěcená

IS THIS REALLY the right way? she asked herself.

Pavla said something.

"What?" Lenka looked at her, leaving the landscape to the darkness without trying to figure out what might be hiding behind the trees and the subtle haze.

"You asked whether we were going the right path, so I say we are."

"Did I say it out loud?"

"Obviously." Pavla rolled her eyes and continued to look ahead so as not to lose touch with the road, which Lenka found quite easy—a narrow road, trees on the right, the surface of the pond on the left.

"Are you really sure?"

"I told you I wasn't here for the first time, didn't I? You fool, look at yourself." Pavla shook her head. "Instead of looking forward to turning off and enjoying relaxation, you're frightened off from a forest path that . . . Where do you actually think it leads? To the hell's maw?"

Pavla laughed and Lenka folded her arms grimly across her chest, though her eyes kept peeking out, as if something could really come out of the darkness.

"Look," Pavla continued, "this place is secluded. Maybe a former hunting lodge or something. But it's definitely not like we're in the wilderness. There should be peace, nothing should disturb you. That's all. And you need it as hell. You're still tense like if you can't switch off."

"I can't do that either. But I would like to see—"

"Yes, I know, you'd like to see me handle it in your place; but in the first place, I wouldn't be at work, where more and more tasks come to me every day and they still think they deserve praise that they have raised your gross wages by a thousand crowns in the last year. They should go fuck themselves. Honestly, I can't understand you working there for almost ten years."

Lenka felt that on the road, they would not be able to avoid the oncoming car, as it was narrow, moreover lined with trees on both sides. The pond disappeared, and their little Hyundai was surrounded only by the forest and a kind of light from the top of the gentle hill they were heading for.

"Maybe it'll be fine," she said at last.

"Damn it, it's gonna be great! Sauna, hot tub, massage from a masseur . . ."

"Come on!" She slapped Pavla lightly on the back of her hand on the gear knob.

"What? You're going to relax here, but I don't know why you shouldn't enjoy it a little more. You will forget and stretch more than just muscles."

"You're crazy." Lenka shook her head, blushing.

"I'm not crazy, I'm just happy to be able to relax."

"And did you and the masseur . . . "

"No, but he gave me the number that I could call for a massage because he's from town."

"And did you?"

"No, I have my own resources, I didn't need this one. Plus, he was a little old for me."

"I forgot you're a cougar." Lenka smirked.

"Look, I would go with the older one, but at my age, I just like it for some reason when the guy below me looks like he just finished high school and doesn't really know what to do with his life. Probably some kind of maternal complex. And he should have a figure of an athlete. The older ones don't have that anymore. Although, if I remember correctly, this masseur still looked very good."

Lenka inhaled as if she would say something else, as if awakening in her the Catholic upbringing she had learned from American television series, but Pavla did not allow her to speak.

"And here we are," she said sharply, guiding the car to a small parking lot. The clock read less than five o'clock. It was as dark as midnight. However, the area was lit. "So," Pavla continued as she locked the car, "now leave everything here. We go to the reception, check in there, get our bathrobes and towels, get our things from the car, go to our room, then for a small dinner and until nine to the spa center. I want to go to the sauna, I want to warm up, I want to go to the hot barrel, and I don't want you to protest."

"I didn't even plan to," Lenka said resignedly.

"I like you that way." Pavla sent her friend an airy kiss, having the door at the reception held by a handsome young man. She couldn't do otherwise and had to smile lovingly at him.

* —⋅—✦—⋅— *

Pavla was surprised how full the restaurant was. It never happened that she would come inside and not find a single free table.

The waiter headed for them immediately. "Good evening, ladies. I'm very sorry, but we're a little crowded right now." He threw up his hands. "If you would be willing to wait half an hour, for example to go to the sauna, it will definitely clear up a bit. We have a private event in the lounge, and there is a bit of pressure."

"Let's go," Lenka wanted to say, inhaling, but her friend overtook her.

"What about there?" She pointed to the table for four, where only a pair of young men sat. They enjoyed the appetizer.

The waiter smiled. He left to fill out their request. At one point, the faces of the two young men turned to Lenka to see who was asking them to sit down. She felt she blushed again. She had to avert her eyes. On the contrary, Pavla returned the gaze to the young men calmly, almost defiantly. The men at the table turned back to each other, shrugged, then the one closer to the door said something to the waiter, who bowed and walked over to the waiting women.

"I would like to quote the young man directly. He said he would be honored if you honored them with your presence at their table."

Pavla looked so excited that Lenka was afraid that her friend would start shaking like a hen in front of roosters.

Martin Štefko

The waiter beckoned to them, and they followed. Pavla aimed straight at the place opposite the entrance to the restaurant, as if she wanted to make sure that no one new would escape her. Lenka did not object. She sat down next to the thin man, who was watching her curiously. He had a high forehead and no thick hair, but not that he was bald in two years. He might have been twenty-five, maybe a little less—confused by the wrinkles in the corners of his mouth that made dimples in his face, though he wasn't smiling. He had piercing blue eyes that she couldn't bear to look straight into.

"We are very grateful to you." Pavla tore the thorn from her heel as she caught the attention. "We already thought we would freeze outside until a table became available."

"After all, you could really warm up in the sauna," the man next to Lenka returned to her.

"I'd have to undress, and it's too early for that." Pavla smiled as if nothing had happened.

"The right time will surely come." The tall young man winked at her.

Lenka would have sat better next to another man, smaller, at first glance more diffident, with a small, round face and a beginning belly. Instead of having a conversation, the man drank tea and slowly continued his salad with pieces of cheese. After a while, Lenka received her own plate of salad, followed by a creamy fish soup. They chose the main course from two dishes. Either carp with tarhoni salad, which she immediately rejected, she didn't have to have so many fish, or grilled cutlet with mashed potatoes. Pavla remained faithful to the fish and had a carp.

Lenka ate slowly and kept her eyes on the other

guests, staff, and equipment. Relaxation in a nutshell, as Pavla said. She'd talked about this place for a long time, so Lenka let herself be persuaded. She needed a shutdown.

＊ ━━━ ▌ ━━ ＊

As soon as the two men finished the last course, they said goodbye.

"What do you say?" she asked Pavla.

"Yeah, I like it here."

"But I don't mean this," Pavla waved. "I mean the two of them. There is something that can be done about them, right?"

"You may like the youngsters, but I don't."

"Please, they're not such youngsters."

"They're about ten years younger."

"So you see, they couldn't be your sons anymore."

"You're really stupid."

"Can I get you something else, ladies?" the waiter interjected.

"No, thank you," they agreed.

"Will you pay at the departure?"

"Yes, at four," Pavla said.

"Have a nice evening, ladies," he said.

Pavla got up as if on command, and Lenka followed her. There was still noise in the next lounge, and even in the main area, it didn't seem like it was just being harvested.

"He would be worth sin too, wouldn't he?" Pavla leaned over to Lenka's ear.

"And who?"

"The waiter."

Lenka shook her head. "Listening to you is like you didn't have a guy for two years."

"See, it's been two days, and I miss it."

"I don't."

"Then you're just kidding."

"Not really." Lenka held the door for her friend. They went outside, where it looked like morning frosts according to the temperature and fog.

"You're kidding," Pavla led her. "Or no guy has done it to you like you have something to miss. Well, maybe we can fix it here."

"Ha-ha."

"Just don't laugh."

"We are here only for two days."

"Things can be done in two days. And several times."

"Don't you know me at all? I'm not going with someone for one night."

"It doesn't have to be a night, it can be a day." Pavla laughed.

"I guess I'm starting to regret going with you."

"But please don't be such a climber. Now we go to the room, just put on a bathrobe and show tits in the wellness. You never know who will catch them."

"Probably a mouse due to gravity."

Pavla laughed throatly. "You're stupid!"

"I'm not, that's a fact."

"Never mind, these youngsters are catching at an older woman who has experience."

"I have none—"

"Oh, just shut up already," Pavla cut her off. "We're just going to undress and see what's going on. If nothing else, we just relax. This will also help. And tomorrow, you will have a massage and get a little wet."

"You're stupid."

Pavla just grimaced as she struggled a little, eventually successfully, with an electronic lock in the room.

— ——✦—— —

Lenka had her swimsuit packed, but at Pavla's insistence, she only went in a bathrobe. And since the wellness area was a separate building, which they could reach from the apartment house after about fifty meters in the icy air, it was a quick walk. Among other things, because they had a room upstairs, where they could be reached by a metal staircase, it showed too many of the people below them that they had not taken underwear. Lenka tried to run down the stairs as fast as possible without killing herself. It didn't help when Pavla assured her that no one would see her friend in this darkness anyway.

"Look, I'll give you a guide now," Pavla said, as the door closed behind them. "There are locker rooms here at the beginning, men's lockers there, but we don't care much about them, do we? We're going to women's. Will you keep something there?"

"I have a swimsuit," she raised her hand.

Pavla rolled her eyes. "Then feel free to go there. But otherwise, you probably don't have to put anything in there." They moved out to the hall. "There are stairs up there, we're not interested in them yet, but tomorrow, we are. There are massages. We could still buy some procedures, but we'll see how it gets full."

"What procedures? Like a Scottish jet shower?"

"Have it at the bar," Pavla laughed at her own joke. "A little bit of mud, relaxing aromatherapy, something like that. Actually, I was just in the mud, I usually go just for massages. I'd rather be down here in the warmth, where the people are. It's so lonely up there." She opened the door and held it for her friend. There was a hot tub right in the first room.

"They have a swimsuit!" Lenka whispered.

"They are different kind. Don't pay attention to them." They walked past the hot tub and the toilet door. "There are showers, there is a rest area, here is a sauna and steam."

"What is this?" Lenka pointed to two small pools.

"Kneipp path. One is hot water, the other is cold."

"And what is it good for?"

"I have no idea." Pavla continued.

"Are we going out again?"

"Of course. There's another sauna over there," Pavla said as the cold outside air blew on them both. "And then there's the best thing."

"What is that?"

"Barrels with hot water. Like, it's really hot, about forty degrees. You will immerse yourself in them."

"And that's good for what?"

"How am I supposed to know? You're just loaded with hot water, naked, and you probably hope that a guy climbs in to warm you up in the evening. Or he'll start teasing you with his big toe."

"What kind of world do you live in?!" Lenka was horrified.

"Beautiful one. Try it sometime. What would you like to try first?"

"I don't know, you're like at home here."

"Okay, the barrel is busy, so we take a shower and warm up a little in the steam. It will put you in a good mood for saunas, your pores and such nonsense will open up."

"So you see you know something about that."

"Just what the first person I was here with told me. Crazy for sauna and such, but I didn't listen much. He talked a lot, and it turned out to be boring me."

"Then why were you with him?"

"Because he was a guy with whom, when you sleep, you know that sex isn't just about some jerk piercing you like a chicken on a barbecue, but you'll both enjoy it."

"Are you serious?" slipped Lenka before she could stop it.

Pavla looked at her condescendingly, tilted her head, and stroked her friend's cheek. "My little one." She quickly withdrew her hand, her expression roughening again. "Now take off your bathrobe, take a shower, and we're going to steam. By the way, watch out where you're sitting."

"Sure, so I don't accidentally sit in someone's lap, do I?"

Pavla looked at her with a smile that didn't contain a bit of humor. "No, if you sit too close to the steam generator, it could burn you."

◆────◆────◆

The dry air in the sauna made every breath uncomfortable, at least in the beginning, but she quickly realized that she was safe. Although she felt she was overcoming a panic attack at first, she eventually lasted perhaps ten minutes, her body soaked with sweat. Pavla also had enough for a start and went with her, she didn't even flirt with a man with a high hat on his head, on which was said: Made in USSR.

"What's the pool for?" Lenka asked as they climbed out of the sauna.

"To cool off."

"Ah, but it says that the water temperature is ten degrees."

"Just try it," Pavla urged, not showing anything. But she laughed inwardly.

Lenka shrugged, hung the sheets on a hanger, and climbed naked up the steps. She descended confidently to the first one, so she dipped her foot down to her ankle. A thoughtful look appeared on her face. To Pavla's surprise, she finally immersed herself. It was as if nothing had happened, she climbed out and wrapped herself in a bathrobe.

Pavla just stared at her friend with her mouth open and her hands turned palms in a gesture "What the hell is going on?"

"I guess I'm hardy." Lenka shrugged.

"I didn't go there by any mistake. All I had to do was dip my finger. I was waiting for you to start screaming. You . . . "

"Surprised?"

"I meant disappointed, but yeah, you definitely have good points."

"But now I would take a hot shower."

"Yeah, and we'll lie down for a while, take a breath. Then we'll go to the barrel."

"It doesn't look like it's been free since we arrived."

"Let's just wait then. I want in that barrel. It's beautiful in there."

"But I will not touch you there."

"You don't have to," Pavla grinned. "I'll touch you."

Lenka wanted to laugh, but suddenly, she wasn't so sure that her friend was kidding.

———◆———

"Ahhh," Pavla breathed as she finally loaded herself into a hot barrel whose water temperature was almost exactly 40 ° C.

Lenka quickly plunged after her. As she'd walked naked toward the barrel, she felt as if everyone from the glass restroom was watching her. She was a little afraid of how the hot water would affect her, but she felt good. Very well, actually. She sat down opposite to Pavla, just her head above the surface, and closed her eyes.

"It's fine, isn't it?" said Pavla.

"Definitely so. I have no idea why I've never been to a similar center."

"Yeah, you look like a sauna maid."

"Not anymore," Lenka grinned.

"I'm glad your first time is with me," Pavla returned to her.

They both paused. They were fine. They didn't mind at all that the air temperature was around zero. The steam from the heated barrel warmed their faces. Winter did not reach them.

"So, how's the water?" A male voice suddenly asked, and Lenka needed to cover herself immediately, because he had come only to watch her or worse! The gray-haired athletic man was smiling at them. He reached into the water for something.

Lenka wanted to start screaming.

Martin Štefko

He fished out a thermometer.

"Temperature beautiful," the man said, smiling again. He didn't seem to be staring. Then he walked over to the back of the barrel, where the stove was smoking, and said, "Let's add a little so it doesn't go out." He finished his task, smiled again, and left.

"I mean, I was scared." Lenka breathed as if she'd been holding her breath the whole time.

"That's him." Pavla raised an eyebrow defiantly.

"Who is he?"

"That masseur."

"The . . . the good looking one, or what did you say?"

"Yeah. He'll do it for you tomorrow."

"What will he do to me ?!" Lenka exclaimed.

"The massage." Pavla winked at her. "But he's handsome, what do you mean?"

"Ha-Ha. I was really scared that he was a pervert."

"Let him look. You should feel good that someone wants to see you naked. You're still worth it."

"I don't find it so much fun."

"Because you're too . . . " But Lenka didn't get to know what it was. Another male appeared near their barrel.

"Do you need something?" Pavla smiled at them in a friendly and unequivocal affection.

Lenka turned. Young men from dinner. Now they wore no warm clothing, only exposed bathrobes and towels around their waists.

"I feel a bit embarrassed," he said, the taller and more handsome, "but wouldn't you like to return the favour from dinner? We have been here for about three hours, and so far, we have not been able to get into the barrel."

"Would you like to join us?" Pavla asked.

"If you don't mind." The young man shrugged apologetically. The other stood shyly behind him.

Pavla looked at Lenka.

Lenka took a breath to object.

Pavla just nodded and looked back at the young men. "I think there is enough space. Neither of us will have a problem with you. Our barrel is your barrel."

Lenka rolled her eyes at Pavla, but she pretended not to see her. Instead, she moved to make room for new visitors. Lenka rose to climb out, but about a meter away a penis appeared, causing her to roar back into the water.

"We'll fit in beautifully," Pavla said as the men settled down and everything could be seen in the calm water under the dim but adequate lighting.

"I think so. When we meet like this—and we will probably still meet—I am Milan," the taller of the young men introduced the conversation.

"Pavla." She shook his hand, rising so that her nicely shaped artificial breasts would rise above the surface.

"Lenka." She didn't shake hands and remained submerged.

"This is Honza." Milan pointed at his companion, who shook hands with Pavla and just smiled knowingly at Lenka.

"Did you come today?" Pavla asked.

"A moment before of you," Milan replied.

"How long will you stay?"

"Two nights. We have a package from some flash sales."

Pavla just laughed. She didn't shop at some flash sales. "Did you come to relax before the holidays?"

"Something like that," Milan agreed. "We're from IT, we've had enough work over a year, we're still sitting at the computer, and you like to drop out."

"I see. We could probably say we're office rats too."

"Do you work together?"

"We used to work together, but I like new challenges. Lenka is a stalwart, but since we worked together, we have stayed in touch, and we will go somewhere here and there."

"You couldn't have chosen this place better."

"I come here every year," Pavla confirmed.

"So you know it well here." Milan slapped into the water, and it splashed. "I'm sorry, I was just pleased. There is incredible peace here. But I've already found that two nights is enough. Man is regenerated like never before."

"My words. Yeah, and I guess we be on first-name terms."

"Sure, I'm sorry. It's just that in our job, we have to . . . " The words faded away, and Milan hoped that none of the women would guess what he wanted to say. Rather, he changed the subject. "If you've been coming here for some time, do you remember what it was like with towels at the beginning?"

Pavla nodded. "A pile of them was laid out in a room with a whirlpool. Everyone could take as many as they needed."

"Exactly. And gradually, it began to change. At first, each received a towel for himself and a sheet for the sauna, which he could easily throw in the locker room when he left. And now, this is not even the case, everything has to be handed over when leaving the reception."

"Why?" Lenka interjected.

Her friend looked at her as if she saw a kitten dying by the road and she knew there was nothing she could do about it. "Because people stole them."

"Why would anyone steal a towel?"

Milan smiled. "You can see that you're looking at it from your point of view. You would never steal a towel. But there are people who, when they see a chance to appropriate something without paying, go for it."

"It's still a theft," Lenka continued in disbelief.

"Excuse her," Pavla said to Milan, "but she's very naive sometimes."

"There's nothing wrong with that, but one should know how it works, what kind of people they are. It's a theft, but who can prove to them that they took it? Even if they call their house from the hotel, the thieves will deny it."

"That's terrible." Lenka shook her head.

"Not terrible, it just shows that people are just ruthless. And then others who would normally follow the rules will pay for it. But do you want to hear one funny story?"

"I'm all ears," Pavla smiled.

So far, Lenka had put together a picture of people who visit the resort. It never occurred to her that there would be towel thieves among those she saw. Pavla was right, she looked at the world naively here and there. She heard that people could kill basically every day, but that someone was stealing towels . . . She probably didn't expect people to do such nonsense.

"I've heard," Milan began, "that the owner is kinda pissed off about this towel problem."

"I'm not surprised," Pavla snorted.

"So he thought he would do something about it," Milan continued, pretending that he was telling now, and he didn't want anyone to disturb him. Pavla understood. "So, in addition to taking the precautions I was talking about—reducing the number of towels per guest, having to return them to the reception—he introduced another improver. A tracking device is sewn into each towel, a simple locator that determines the exact position of the towel. So they can always track down thieves."

"That's bullshit!" Pavla made herself clear. "We would know if there was something in the towel."

"Really?" Milan looked at her from under his eyebrows. "Today's technologies—and I kind of know what I'm talking about—have miniaturization as one of the main stages of development. It's not really that complicated to create a simple GPS locator."

"And what about its reach?"

Milan tapped his index finger and middle finger to his temple. "Correctly, the reach of such device wouldn't be great. But it is enough for someone to watch when the guests leave, if a towel also leaves with them. Someone is sitting at the computer checking this."

"It's bullshit!" Pavla laughed. "What would they do then?"

"They'll note who's leaving with the towel, and since they have his address, they'll find it."

"They'll find him and . . . "

"They'll find him and get the towel back. At any cost."

Pavla sputtered.

"I can imagine the scenario." Milan laughed, Honza smirking beside him. "They knock on the door, hands in their pockets. 'We're here for the towel you stole from us.' 'I don't know about any towels.' 'The towel has a locator in it. We can find it in your apartment with an accuracy of one centimeter.' 'I don't know anything.' And so on and so forth. And if by chance the thief didn't get his mind, they would break into his apartment, maybe push him a little against the wall, and then just take the towel. Justice is served, and the resort has lost one of its clients."

"It could be a pretty good mob movie," Honza added.

"Offer it to Scorsese. Now he finished *The Irishman*, so maybe he will throw himself into this," suggested Pavla.

All three laughed. And Lenka joined them. She wasn't laughing out loud, she was just smiling. She didn't mind sitting here with two naked men she didn't know and who weren't born when she went to third grade. She dipped her whole body, closed her eyes, and felt how warm the water was, how pleasant it was, that her head was a little dizzy. She should have a drink because the sauna and all procedures were dehydrating, but she just had nothing at hand and did not intend to drink water from the barrel. She let herself be carried away by the waves and realized that she was not thinking about anything, nothing was bothering her. She was just enjoying herself and, even if she didn't admit it at first, the nudity and the freedom associated with it. No boyfriend—ex!—who never had time for her and eventually reprimanded her for walling up their relationship. No vision of holidays with parents. Sure, to be with them on the first day of Christmas, why not, but on Christmas Eve? At her age? No, she imagined Christmas differently. There was none of that in the barrel. Everything disappeared for a while. She didn't expect the days at the resort to help her soul, but she seemed to take off some of what was bothering her with her clothes. *You will have to pay more attention to sauna and relaxation. Why do not pay more attention for yourself?*

Pavla's voice tore her from the peace and quiet. "I'm already warm. I'm going to rest. Are you coming too?"

But Lenka didn't want to. Suddenly, she liked the barrel. "I'll be . . . I'll be here for a while," she said to herself, surprisingly brave, fully aware that she would be alone in the bath with two men.

Pavla smiled warmly at her and hissed, "Just relax, honey." Then she stood up, showing a surprisingly firm body. Her ass stood out beautifully on top of the barrel. Then she disappeared from sight.

Lenka just smiled at her companions and closed her eyes. She did not allow herself to be disturbed by her contemplation. The men didn't talk either. The silence was ghostly. Silence that can exist in a group of people. There are three, but they can be side by side without disturbing each other's private words. Lenka wanted to share this fact. She opened her eyes to say what had occurred to her, how nice it was that they could coexist in such peace, but the words froze in her. Milan and Honza were kissing.

Milan noticed that Lenka was looking at them.

How can he keep his eyes open when kissing? she thought. She should have shut her's up.

The young men detached from each other. "I guess we'll be leaving too." Milan was staring into his friend's eyes now.

"Maybe to the room already," Honza suggested.

"I'm sure we'll see each other again," she said quickly.

As they emerged from the barrel, she did not look at them, staring at the wooden structure of the container, which suddenly emptied. Lenka was left alone. And it suited her. But she already felt soggy. She closed her eyes. Just for a minute.

She didn't even notice how the space around her had emptied. Nobody went to the barrel, nobody used the pool, and the sauna was empty.

Lenka heard a clatter.

She thought someone tripped. She wasn't excited.

The rumble sounded again.

She realized that it was not coming from a wellness area, but from a forest.

The noise came again, as if something was about to attract attention.

Lenka opened her eyes.

She froze a little, even though her body was sunk in hot water. She realized that she was alone, that the only thing that sounded was rumbling. Fear told her not to look at the sound, reason said it too, but curiosity won out. What if it's a pervert? She would make him a scene such that he would never come gape again.

She looked at the forest.

And she breathed a sigh of relief.

A doe huddled among the bushes and small trees. It probably ran away from the herd, attracted by the smells or the noise. *No, that's stupid*, Lenka thought. Doe would not follow the noise of people. Lenka turned to look at the animal, so that her head was supported on the edge of the barrel. She remembered unconsciously her vacation in Egypt, looking at the sunset like this from the pool, alone because he had to be in the room and finish something on the computer. She was still a bit symbolically alone, Pavla left her here and so did the two gay young men.

The doe had interesting curved horns. A little to the sides, not back.

Horns? flashed in Lenka's head. But doe do not have horns. They have antlers. And do they have antlers at all? Don't only male deers have them?

She wiped her eyes with her fingers.

The animal, whether a doe or not, was looking at her. It stared at her. But not scared. Not with the fact that during its slight movement it should run and disappear into the depths of the forest. It examined her.

There was something wrong with the deer's eyes. As if they weren't animal, as if they were . . .

Goat! Lenka realized. *The animal is more like a goat than a deer. But what would a goat do in the woods? That she would wander to someone?*

Perhaps to confirm her words, the animal took a few short steps and found itself in the open space. A surprisingly massive body was revealed. Bigger than a goat should have.

"What are you?" Lenka said aloud, feeling an unexpected, though certainly not unpleasant, pressure in her lower abdomen.

And it gave her the answer. Unambiguous, though incomprehensible. Simple, yet scary.

It wasn't until he began to rise to the back that she realized that his front limbs were hands all the time. He moved jerkily, his hind legs a little uncertain.

Lenka opened her mouth wide.

About twenty meters away, perhaps less, stood a man with a goat's head, his head so big it became impossible for her to think of a doe first. This was not a doe. He wasn't even an ordinary goat. Opposite her stood a two-meter creature swaying lightly on a goat's feet. He was breathing hard, and steam was coming out of his nostrils.

Lenka closed her mouth without a word. She couldn't even move, she couldn't run, she was just watching.

And then her gaze slid lower.

She gasped at the dimensions of his genitals. That jolted her. Penis protruded toward her like a spear, thick, swollen, and certainly not a goat, human, only of dimensions she considered anatomically impossible.

She hit her back on the barrel. She didn't even realize she was backing away.

She tried to look away from the huge, throbbing penis. He aimed at her, straight at her. As if he wanted to kill her, pierce her through. And she believed the creature could do it.

She fumbled with her hands behind her.

She felt the railings of the steps.

She finally managed to break the connection. She looked away. She could still see the penis, inhuman, burned into the retina or into the inner sight.

She turned and swung up the steps.

She heard heavy, slow breathing behind her.

Martin Štefko

She tried to get down as quickly as possible.

What if he came after her? What if he was already running? What if he wanted to stab her?

Her leg slipped.

She still held on to the railing.

She fell.

The hand slipped.

She landed.

Fortunately, it was not from a great height. It didn't hurt much either.

Darkness spread around.

* —— * —— *

She woke up in a moment. At least that's how it seemed to her. Nothing had changed. No one came to her.

She got up.

Her hand ached a little because she spun as she slipped. She should have let go earlier. But it probably prevented an even worse fall.

She felt her head with her uninjured arm. No, her blood didn't flow. She probably wouldn't even have a bulge.

She managed to get up. Still naked. She went for a towel. When she'd wiped a little, she put on her robe. She tied it up.

She remembered in horror the creature on the edge of the forest.

She turned.

He would be behind her! He would definitely be behind her!

There was no sign of him.

Escaped?

Was he hiding?

Or did it all just seem to her? She was overheated from the water and just dreamed of something so . . . bizarre?

She entered the wellness area and headed straight for the shower. She looked forward to the cold water that would wake her. She was slack from the barrel and also from the fall. Not that she was loitering, but she didn't feel completely in her skin. And then that hallucination.

She let the water fall on her. With a smile, she took a shower longer than necessary. The cold woke her. She felt better. Only the hand still hurt.

She wiped herself in a towel, wrapped herself in a bathrobe, and went to bed in the rest area.

She only found Pavla there. She was lying on one of the loungers, her eyes closed. The restroom was otherwise empty.

Lenka threw the sheet on the couch next to Pavla and settled down on her own. She just lay down, reached out, closed her eyes, and was glad she didn't have to do anything. She liked the wellness, even the memory of the strange meeting disappeared and was no longer so intense.

"You knew that, didn't you?" Lenka broke the silence after a moment.

"Wha-at?" Paul growled. She almost seemed to fall asleep.

"That they are gay," Lenka said.

"Yeah." Pavla smiled. "Didn't you notice Milan squeezing Honza's thigh? I was waiting for him to start jerking him off the underwater."

"Then you could have said something and not left me there alone with them."

Martin Štefko

"I thought you noticed."

"I didn't."

"Besides, I feel like they haven't been there with you for so long."

"Yeah, they went in a minute. You wouldn't believe what happened to me then. I was lying in a barrel and suddenly it came . . . "

<hr/>

Lenka couldn't sleep. Although she told the story to Pavla with the strange goat as amusing, when she turned off the lights, the joke disappeared. The aching hand proved that she felt fear. But now, she was only to blame for her too-wild imagination. A two-meter-high goat standing on its back with a penis perhaps about half a meter? No, she had no idea what might create such an idea.

She turned on her side. Pavla slept peacefully. They had a shared double bed, which sloped a little in the middle, thanks to two mattresses. They could easily have woken up in the morning huddled together. But Lenka would have to fall asleep.

Pavla breathed nicely regularly. She slept in an interesting way. She lay on her back, her hands resting on her stomach. Like on the bier. She looked calm, not radiating in her sleep the cynicism she normally showed. She was beautiful, a little artificial with too pointed a nose, but really beautiful. Even without her makeup.

Lenka reached out to stroke Pavla's cheek.

She quickly withdrew her arm.

What the hell got into her? Stroking her sleeping friend! She must have got tired and started fooling around. Time to go out. She inhaled fresh air and got better again. She no longer felt like stroking Pavla's beautiful face.

Lenka shook her head and sat up quickly.

She thought she was going to get dressed, but in the end, she threw only her bathrobe over her pajamas, still wet as she had walked naked in it.

She quietly sneaked through the room so as not to wake Pavla. And then back again because she forgot the key on the TV table. Eventually, she went out. She wondered if she should lock Pavla in, but in the end, she told herself that it wasn't necessary, that she wouldn't go anywhere anyway, she would just get some air on the steel staircase.

The fresh air, though cold, did her good. Not that she fell asleep right away, but the cold seemed beneficial, she felt that her body was still alive, she just needed to find harmony. Still figure out how.

The view in front of her was not dizzying. Apart from the fact that it was night and a couple of outdoor lamps were on—probably for people like her who couldn't sleep—she only saw the opposite building with the other rooms, turning her head to the left for the reception, to the right for the wellness area. She looked down on both buildings. And what else? Just forest, nothing else. Pine and spruce forest, sometimes a bare deciduous tree.

There was peace outside. Her eyes darted, looking for a goat's head, but the only thing resembling an animal was a wooden statue of an owl on one of the branches of a tree growing between buildings. That linden tree?

She took a deep breath until the cold air stung her nose.

Martin Štefko

She exhaled. And she almost chuckled. She heard something. Familiar sound, albeit inappropriate. Mainly in public. Where did it come from? The sound of a woman enjoying a male penetration. She couldn't be mistaken. And it certainly didn't come out of an open window, this was happening outside.

Lenka found herself descending the steel stairs.

Why? Why was she going down? Would she do this normally?

Whatever moralities raced through her head, she continued to descend, step by step. And the noise seemed to be intensifying, but she didn't know if it was because the couple was already heading for the climax or because she was approaching them.

Why am I going there? she asked herself as she stepped on the solid ground and continued on to the corner of the building, where she heard a hiss.

I'm curious?
Am I horny?
Am I spoiled?
Do I want to stop them?
Do I want to watch?
Do I want to join?

Questions raced through her head, longing for answers. And then all of a sudden, they faded away, and she looked around the corner. She saw exactly what she expected. The woman, relatively young, was leaning forward against the wall, the man entering from behind, until the woman had to use her hands to keep as far away from the wall as possible and not hit her head on it.

Lenka remained mostly around the corner, only her head peeking out.

Go home, an inner voice told her.

She didn't listen. She kept looking.

The man stabbed his whole cock into the woman. He didn't spare her.

Lenka did not look away. She watched the woman's white ass. The man had hairy legs, his pants slid to his ankles. He was holding a T-shirt, his gaze blank, staring at the wall.

The man kept penetrating the woman.

The woman clasped her hands on the wall. She protruded her ass to her lover's movements.

And he pushed again.

Lenka admired how well they were played.

Their pace increased. He was sweating. She moaned louder and louder now.

Lenka realized that her fingers were wet. When she looked at them, she realized why. She hadn't even noticed when she put her hand in her pajama pants and started touching her cleft. It was damp, very damp.

What's wrong with me? her head flashed.

In response, she slid her fingers inside.

She raised her eyes.

He looked at her. He pushed the woman but looked at Lenka.

She was taken aback, but she didn't hide. She didn't even pull her fingers out of her own crotch.

He smiled.

And then his head changed. Suddenly, he was no longer a dark-haired man; she was suddenly looking at a large goat's head. It laughed too.

Lenka covered her mouth with her free hand. But why shouldn't she scream? Why not? It would come in handy right now!

Martin Štefko

The man pulled out of the woman. The human penis suddenly changed in the air. Lenka stared at the terrifying half-meter tool.

The goat grinned at her.

Lenka understood.

She wanted to avert her eyes. She didn't want to watch the sequel.

"Put it there! Put it back!" the woman begged.

Lenka tried to get her eyelids together. But her eyelids didn't obey. As if the subconscious wanted to watch, watch everything that followed. And Lenka saw everything.

"Come on! Put it back!"

And he obeyed.

Lenka bit her lip as she saw the half-meter-thick limb disappear in the woman, who seemed too small for it. Every woman seemed way too small.

The bowed mistress gasped. It sounded differently. Surprised. And in pain. The incredible pain that came to her brain later. She was full like never before. Full as any woman should never be.

He pulled it out, maybe half, and pushed it back.

The woman's hands loosened. Her face hit the wall. But he held her. He didn't let her fall.

Tears streamed down Lenka's cheeks.

He continued. On and on. He kept his eyes on Lenka. Each beat made a disgusting squelching sound. And suddenly, it began to squirt blood from the terrifying connection. The dying mistress's ass was no longer pale but adorned with scarlet. And much more of it was on the raging lover. And on the wall. And on the ground.

Lenka was thankful for the poor lighting. She didn't see everything.

Man—goat!—he began to pound like he was furious.

The woman just hung on his hands.

Finally, the connection of the goat's eyes with Lenka's broke. In an orgasm, he turned his head to the sky and made a sound that resembled a wolf's howl, like a deer trumpeting in a rut.

And then he pulled that cock out of his dead mistress.

But it wasn't just his penis that came out of her.

Her entrails began to slap against the ground. They rushed out in a flood of blood.

Lenka finally gained control of her own body. Despite her teary eyes, she managed to get up the stairs. She ran upstairs, unable to tell how she found herself upstairs, and finally got into the room and locked the door behind her.

She was leaning against the door. Her chest heaved in frantic hopes and outbursts. There were more and more tears streaming down her cheeks. They landed on the bathrobe, on the floor. Her knees gave out. She fell to the ground. Legs twisted under each other. Her hand still in her crotch. She took it out in disgust. She smashed the tiles several times. She didn't even realize the pain. She just angered the previous injury.

She calmed down, albeit very slowly.

She felt her heart pound rapidly just remembering him.

At his gaze.

For how supple the woman was.

To what fell out of her when . . .

Lenka's stomach began to roll. She tried to pick herself up, go to the bathroom. As she leaned against the toilet, she already knew she would not vomit. She choked, everything remained.

Maybe I didn't wake Pavla, she thought, because she realized she was making a lot of noise on the way to the bathroom.

She listened.

There seemed to be silence in the bedroom.

She got up from the toilet and closed the door. She let the water run, let it flow as cold as possible into the sink in a faint trickle, and then filled a bowl out of her palms to splash her face. Water didn't even seem as cold as she froze outside. Only now did she realize how cold her face, arms, and legs were. She leaned against the heating ladder, which was still a little warm. She took off her bathrobe and leaned on the warm poles to warm herself. The construction pressed against her breasts and chin. It suddenly seemed to her that warming up was very important. What happened would go away with the heat. No, she didn't think this trip, this short rest trip Pavla had persuaded her to, was a good idea. It was a very bad idea, perhaps the worst idea Pavla had ever had.

She'd warmed up a little. However, her head did not calm down.

What should she do?

She should call the police.

First of all, she went to check the door.

Locked.

But would it withstand the onslaught of that . . .

creature? She imagined him running, bowing his head, and breaking through the chipboard like a hammer and being here. The goat must have had incredible strength. Just because he could pierce a woman in a single insertion.

Lenka's stomach rolled over again, but just burped again.

What should she do?

The question came back. She wanted to go call the police, but it was as if she couldn't. As if something was stopping her. Perhaps more questions.

Where was her phone?

What was the number on the police?

Would they believe her and come?

How long before they arrived? Wouldn't it be too late?

What if the goat got in yet?

He went after her, she knew. He looked at her. The whole show was for her. She should have enjoyed looking at how . . . he was fucking? How did he kill? What power did he have?

Why her? Why did he choose her?

She went to the bedroom, to Pavla.

Should she wake her up? Consult with her?

Lenka sat on the bed.

Pavla groaned.

"Aren't you sleeping?" Lenka asked eagerly.

There was only another groan in response.

Lenka was worried. As if something hurt her friend. For a moment, she completely forgot about the bloody scene. She turned on a small lamp. Only a faint, warm light spread through the room.

Pavla continued to lie on the bed, on her back,

stretched out like a plank, her hands resting on her stomach.

"Are you all right?" she asked carefully.

No, Pavla couldn't be all right. Her face was twisted in a painful grimace, all her wrinkles deepening. Her teeth were gritted as she tried not to scream.

"Pavla, what's wrong with you?" Lenka leaned over, as if she could only relieve her friend with a closer look in her eyes.

"My . . . be . . . lly . . . " she managed to get out.

"Does your stomach hurt?"

"So . . . much!" A tear came from her eye.

"How . . . how can I help you? I got you . . . Do you want a drink? Any pill? Should I call an ambulance?" Again, so many questions, as if she couldn't answer any and needed someone else to decide for her, even a friend in terrible pain.

"Just . . . look . . . look . . . there . . . "

"On your stomach?" Lenka asked stupidly.

"Yeeees!" Pavla shouted. She no longer held her teeth together, and some of the pain left her without helping.

"Okay, okay," Lenka tried to reassure her, stroking her cheek. Then she grabbed the tip of the blanket that covered Pavla. She slowly pulled it down. Pavla slept naked. Lenka was not even surprised by the fact. She felt pressure in her lower abdomen.

What the hell is wrong with me?!

She didn't understand herself anymore. How could she feel excitement at such a moment? A gentle shiver flooded her gut. She couldn't command it, she couldn't stop it.

She returned to Pavla.

She removed the blanket from her belly.

Lenka cried out in fright. She bounced off her friend. She lost her balance. She landed hard on the ground with her ass. Eyes staring at Pavla.

"Oh my God! Oh my God! Oh my God!" she repeated softly.

The bed was high, she could not see Pavla from the ground.

What if everything she saw—a goat, his fellowship, and now uncovered Pavla—was just a dream? How could that be a fact?!

She knelt to see better.

No. Nothing seemed to her! Nothing!

Pavla could not reveal herself because her hands grew into her stomach. It lacked the flatness that Pavla was proud of. Her muscles disappeared beneath what Lenka could only perceive as a soaking scab. The whole abdomen was strewn with a brownish-yellow bark structure, under which something was moving.

"Pavla," Lenka breathed, tears in her eyes.

Her friend did not react, she kept her teeth clamped together.

"What is it?"

At one point, a sore burst, from which a pus-like fluid spurted. There was a smell in the room. This time, Lenka puked. The vomit ended up on the floor at her knees. She covered her mouth with a hand, smelling the stomach juices in her mouth, but even those could not overcome the disgustingly sweet yet bitter odor of Pavla's body.

"Don't worry, don't worry," she tried to say, but rather mumbled to herself. "I'll call for help."

She looked at her friend once more. Another sore seemed to be about to erupt, so she quickly scrambled to her feet, ripped the phone from the charger, and ran through the hall to the hallway. It didn't occur to her that the goat could be waiting for her there. And he wasn't. The hallway in front of the room was empty, and the door to the steel stairs was not open either. He wasn't following her.

This time, she closed it behind her. She didn't want to smell the stink.

She managed to unlock the phone only after several attempts because she placed the thumb of her other hand on the fingerprint reader. Even though she had experienced the gesture for a year using her mobile phone, she suddenly still used the wrong hand. Maybe because her right hand was beating in pain.

She opened the call app and tapped 112. She put the phone to her ear. After a while, it said, "The number you called does not exist."

"What?" She didn't understand. It must have been mistaken.

She looked at the screen.

112.

Probably a mistake.

She erased the number and rewrote it.

112.

"The number you have dialed does not exist."

So, she tried another one, 158.

"The number you have dialed does not exist."

155

"The number you have dialed does not exist."

150.

"The number you have dialed does not exist."

"What the fuck is going on?!"

She dumbly tried 911.

"The number you have dialed does not exist."

Lenka tried to call her mom.

"The number you have dialed does not exist."

"Shit!" she shouted at the phone, but since she didn't have an iPhone, Siri couldn't tell her anything. "Shit! Shit!"

What now? The phones obviously didn't work. She had a full signal, but none of her numbers existed, which, of course, was nonsense. Probably a mistake. With a useless phone in her right hand, she stood up and knocked on the nearest door with her uninjured hand. She put her forehead on the door with her eyes closed. It wasn't until a few seconds later that she realized that there was no point in knocking on her own room for help.

Yes, she would sleep now. Now she was tired, just when she needed it the least!

She moved to the next door. She knocked. Then she noticed that it had a "STUFF ONLY" sign next to it.

"Shit!" She slammed the door once more.

She tried the ones next door.

Room number 3.

She pounded and waited a moment.

Nothing.

Room number 2.

Nothing.

Room number 1.

Nothing.

"Fuck! Is anybody awake! I need help!" She began

pounding on the door of room number 1, as if trying to kick it out. And then she just leaned against it and broke into tears. She slapped her hand a few more times, but without strength. She ran out of options and didn't know what to do anymore. She couldn't get out. Not alone. There he waited . . .

Did she dream it, or did she hear a noise from behind the door? As if someone was moving there. As if . . .

It clicked in the lock. Someone unlocked. The door opened to a small crack so she could only see an eye.

"Yes?" asked a strangely muffled male voice she didn't recognize right away.

"My friend . . . something happened to her. I need help!"

There was a moment of silence on the other side. Then the voice said, "I'm sorry, but we're asleep."

He wanted to close, but Lenka literally fell onto the door, not letting it just slam in her nose. They burst in together. She knocked down the man to the ground, holding herself on her feet as she grabbed the doorknob that slammed against the wall.

"I just need . . . " Her words faded as she noticed Honza lying on the ground in front of her. All naked. A faint light came from the bedroom. Honza was naked, his skin stained with dark liquid, mostly on his face.

"What happened to you?" she asked stupidly.

It was enough to take two steps and look into the room. Milan lay tied to the bed. Legs and arms outstretched. Blood dripped from where his penis used to be. He was smiling.

"Hello!" he shouted at Lenka. "You wouldn't

believe how it squirts out of a guy when you bite off his cock."

Something in her head understood that she would not find help here, but her body did not obey. So she just stood watching Milan bleed and slowly stop laughing.

Honza rose from the ground. "You know," he stood right in front of her, "I guess I shouldn't just let you go when you've seen this."

"What?" She didn't understand the threat.

"What would happen if I bit your nipples and clit? Do you think that you would bleed too? I would definitely need less strength for that than for biting Milan's dick. You wouldn't believe how much I had to tear."

"And for the time being, I roared as if he couldn't," Milan said cheerfully, though it was clear that his words were losing energy.

"No," Lenka said.

"I think . . . " But he didn't finish the sentence, he looked somewhere behind Lenka.

She started to back away from him.

Honza also took a few steps, surprisingly away from her, not toward her. He was still looking behind her.

Lenka's hips bumped into something. To something hard.

She turned.

She started screaming before she looked into the human eyes in the animal's head.

<hr/>

She woke up. So she had fallen asleep. Or fainted.

She was not wearing any clothes. Still, she didn't feel cold.

Martin Štefko

She opened her eyes.

She lay on a plank terrace between barrels of hot water. Pavla lay beside her. Her belly was open. The scab disappeared and her cavity was exposed. The entrails continued to work, moving as if they were living their own lives. Pavla's expression didn't change, she still seemed to be suffering.

"The water is hot," she heard behind her.

She turned. Milan looked at her from one barrel. He hadn't bled to death yet. Instead, he blushed, blistering on his skin. The water didn't boil, but it must have been very hot. She turned to the other barrel. For some reason, she supposed Honza would be in there. She was wrong. The barrel looked empty.

There was a new sound behind her. Something heavy hit the wooden floor.

She didn't have to turn around to know what it was. Still, she turned.

He stood behind her at of all his imposing height, a huge dick sticking out just above her head. It would be enough to reach out and lean on him if she wanted to get up. Instead of getting up, she pulled away. She didn't make a sound, but her face was terrified.

He looked down at her in his goat form. His massive hairy chest tensed with slow breathing. He snorted here and there. And he just kept looking at her. His cock protruded forward as if he knew nothing but fullness.

Lenka opened her mouth, but no voice came out.

The goat suddenly began to move. He crossed behind the barrel and picked up something from the ground. Lenka stared at the huge ax with an incredibly long blade. She wanted to ask what he wanted to do, but apart from the fact that not a single sound came out of her, the creature immediately showed her what he intended.

He stepped over Pavla, stepped with his hooves several times. Then he swung and cut off the woman's head. It rolled a short distance across the terrace to stop in front of Lenka. She stared at her. Pavla's expression changed from painful to reconciled. A small squeak escaped Lenka, nothing more.

Goat walked over to the barrel. He placed a huge palm on Milan's head and dipped it. Lenka saw Milan's hand waving goodbye above the surface, then it disappeared as well.

The Goat dropped his ax until it rang. He stood against Lenka. She was all too aware that she was alone. Alone. Naked. With him . . . with that.

"Help," her mouth tried to form an unnecessary plea that no one would have heard.

The Goat fell to his knees in front of her. Was there something humble in that gesture? His hair was gray and white, thin in some places, scarred here and there. His body, however, remained firm despite his apparent age, his erection unbreakable.

"Who are you?" she asked.

He did not answer.

She felt a strange weakness, so she lay down. She stared at the sky. It was black and full of stars.

Her only companion growled.

Her legs were crouched, holding them tight.

Looking at the dark heavens, everything else ceased to exist. Just her and the universe. The fear subsided. She forgot about her lover, who had kicked her out just because she stopped amusing him. And maybe she never even started. She forgot the job where she was stuck, had nowhere to go, but knew she would never leave. She envied Pavla, who was now satisfied. And perhaps Milan was satisfied. But what about her? Did she feel dissatisfied? No, now that the fear was gone, when the cosmic emptiness filled it's place, she felt very well. Nothing bothered her, nothing hurt her. Not a hand. Not even a head. Nothing.

A smile spread across her face. She didn't understand where he came from.

It fluttered slightly in her lower abdomen. Nice, natural.

She raised her head a little and looked at the large goat man. He knelt and took a deep breath. His mouth parted a little, a covetous look in his eyes.

Her smile didn't go away. She laid her head again.

The stars were beautiful. So close and so far. She plunged into them. She let them engulf them.

She spread her legs.

Her future lover turned his head and made that sound like a wolf's howl and a deer's trumpet.

She closed her eyes.

And he entered her. She felt as filled as ever. He penetrated every cavity, every cell. The stars may have disappeared from her sight, but she continued to smile at them. Needs she didn't even know she had, had to be fulfilled that night. And she didn't have to worry about anything anymore.

In the end, Pavla was right. She relaxed here like never before.

RITUAL

Petr Boček

Translated by Karolína Svěcená

HE SMILED AND LOOKED happily at his wife's face. It was petite, cute, quiet. This was exactly what he wanted to have for over twenty years. In the phase of initial love, which tangled his head like a handful of skillfully tangled joints, he did consider her nice. Everything changed after the wedding. Not all at once, of course, but gradually. Today he would say that her true nature had begun to be exposed. Domineering, angry, and annoying. When he indicated to her a few times that it was not the same as before, she answered him with a suggestive question: "And do you know for whom?"

He didn't know, there were more options. Maybe because of him, he didn't make much of a career and earned only a little money, almost an alm. He didn't excel in bed, in frequency nor in volume. Besides, he couldn't set up the set-top box or the TV properly, so he faced his wife's diatribes when the image began to part while watching her favorite reality shows. The neighbor had to intervene.

Petr Boček

And that was probably the second reason. A radiant, unrivalled idol from the neighborhood began to visit their apartment, perhaps too often. He could do it. He could do everything. Television has collapsed far too often.

His wife also became physically estranged from him. Her small, formerly cute face was inflated with increasing chins and heraldic cheeks. The bust gradually merged with the abdomen. What did the neighbor see in her? He must have been a lard-lover, otherwise, he couldn't explain it.

His wife was right in one thing. A man should broaden his mental horizons. She once took him to the ethnographic museum. He thought it would be terrible boredom, but he was wrong. He found a display case that caught his eye, and he froze there for an hour and a half while his wife ran through the entire, fairly large exposure. "It was swell," he said to her in such a cheerful tone that it stopped her.

Some primitive tribes, he concluded, came up with great ideas that, although not fully compatible with European culture, are, in some cases, worth following.

When, in about a week, a somewhat confused neighbor came to ask if all the television programs were in order, he told him that he might be surprised, but that they were. "My wife had an excess of life energy," he said to that gigolo, "so it was enough for her to walk past the TV screen and crack! The program immediately transformed into a Cubist image, you know. But somehow, it exhausted her, so she went to Tibet for meditation." Then he slammed the door in front of his neighbor's stunned face.

RITUAL

Of course, he had lied to him. The woman was at home, but she was transformed.

He didn't figure it out himself; the South American Shuars invented it, he just adapted it a little to small-town conditions in Bohemia. They did this to enemies killed in battle, but what else is a non-loving wife but an adversary? How are they different, for God's sake!? Perhaps only because there was no fight. Given her body proportions, he was not going to take any chances.

He poured a fairly large dose of crushed sleeping pills into her Coke. As usual, she drank a full glass at once without a hesitation. She blinked, smirked a little, and said something like she had probably mistakenly bought a fake with an artificial sweetener. Then she walked to the toilet. Nothing happened for a long time, there were no corresponding sounds or rinsing. Then something heavy slumped to the ground. He was ready so he could respond quickly. He opened the door, the victim collapsing at his feet, in fact directly on them, massive elastic pants pulled halfway down the arse. With all his might, he leaned her against the toilet so that the top of her head rested on the toilet seat. He had sharpened his knives in advance, bought a new one just for this so-called ritual occasion. Also, his set of scalpels and balsa-cutters would come in handy. He used them all in the construction of aircraft models before his better half tore off this decent hobby. She called him an overgrown child who was constantly playing and still angry at his parents. But he had acquired enough skill for the fine work that suited him now. Besides, as a child, he used to be a frequent and attentive witness to the gutting of rabbits by his grandfather.

Petr Boček

His wife twitched slightly as he dipped the scalpel into her backside. "Calm down, you bitch!" said the grandfather's former sentence, used in a situation where he had not sufficiently stunned the animal. But like the old man then, he did not allow himself to be distracted. He continued to cut down to the underside of her neck and then around its entire circumference. Although he was very careful, he managed to cut the carotid artery. In a moment, the throat turned into a raging volcano, spewing bloody magma in all directions at regular intervals. There was perhaps no dry place left on him; he could feel the sweet taste of blood in his mouth. Besides, his wife began to grunt wildly.

There was nothing that could be done, he had to immobilize her for good, but not damage the head. He tore her blouse at the chest. He was surprised that he didn't see the nipples, then he realized they must be about forty numbers lower. In his armory, he found the longest knife that would ever be able to penetrate the lard armor. He swung and stabbed. The tip of the knife tinkled against the rib and then slid deeper. He repeated the movement several more times. The body twitched for a moment and then finally stopped moving.

"I should have stabbed you in the first place," he muttered under his breath. "But you have enjoyed it like this, didn't you?"

He continued with a fine work, covered in blood. He carefully trimmed the skin to avoid damaging her face features, keeping the hair in place to keep the ears intact. That was the only part that didn't grow with lard over the years. He kissed them tenderly.

Friday night came, then Saturday morning. He worked for many hours, tirelessly and intensely. His back and eyes ached; his right hand suffered from convulsions several times. However, he was tireless, and the result crowned the work. In the end, he held something in his hand that faithfully resembled a carnival mask with his wife's features.

Now he had to process the meat quickly to keep it from spoiling. He made small portions of it because one person doesn't eat much and he was actually a widower. He put everything carefully in the fridge and the freezer. In those two rich weeks, he had "pork" several times, as he called it. Baked, stewed, cutlets, medallions, and a strong broth. A few times, the liver with onions. He partially flushed the rest of the guts, partly tossed them in plastic bags and carried them to trash cans throughout the town, as well as gnawed bones and a crushed skull.

He took a vacation on Monday and Tuesday, having to work on that artifact. Exactly according to information from the Internet, he cleaned the skin, sewed it with gray thread, and stuffed it with heated sand, stolen from a nearby playground, and a mixture of herbs. He did not know the original composition, so he used lavender, thyme, and oregano. As he dried the restored head in the oven, the smell of soap and pizza took over the apartment. As the artifact gradually shrank, he removed some of the contents until the object reached the size of a clenched fist. That was about fourteen days later. Then he emptied it completely. Tsantsa, as the little head was called by Shuars, was a success. He managed to preserve his wife's appearance, only reducing her to much smaller and cuter size than she ever was. He sewed on her eyelids, those empty holes without eyes looked pretty scary. He kept her mouth open. Unlike the Shuar, he did not believe that any enraged spirit of the sacrifice could emanate through them. If anything like that existed at all, it went away with the rest of the body, which he had almost eaten. And then he had a personal reason to keep the mouth open.

Now he laid the transformed little wife gently on the couch and looked at her fondly. He drank a pleasantly chilled beer. He felt free, as he had not for a long time. He could do whatever he wanted, even throwing alcohol on the carpet without the hail of complaints and threats. He could even light a fire in the living room, get drunk, watch sports broadcasts until midnight. She was so small against him! She was helpless! She was just cute and attractive, even though she lacked most of her body. As soon as he got to the bottom of the bottle, he went to the bathroom. He showered carefully and perfumed himself. He didn't bother dressing. He would have a beautiful romantic evening with his wife.

At first, he was ready to start with foreplay, a recitation of verses or something like that. He knew that before, his wife wouldn't endure it. She had to now. But he could not recall any romantic poem at that moment.

So he went straight to the action. He grabbed the wife's head and put her mouth on his erect penis. It fit exactly, he measured it while drying. Then he began to vibrate with his right hand. A pleasant tingle ran through his body. This was exactly the intimate practice she had always rejected. She had to endure it now, girl. This idea added to his ecstasy.

RITUAL

As the room began to undulate pleasantly before his eyes and the climax approached, he felt a strange pressure below. He looked into his palm. Tsantsa has changed. The threads with which he had stitched her eyes were torn, and two glowing red dots stared at him from the open holes. The pleasure quickly vanished and turned into terror. He tried to quickly break free from the grip of the ritual artifact, but it held him tight and didn't want to let go. It was as if the mouth wrapped around his manhood. Suddenly, dark smoke billowed from his wife's nose. It lit up inside, and his cock was on fire. Literally. He could smell the roasting meat. The pain was so intense that the brain needed to be reset. It darkened before his eyes, and he commanded himself on the carpet.

He didn't wake until dawn. He was still lying on the floor. He remembered his erotic experience and, for a brief moment, thought it must have been a dream. A stupid, crazy dream. Then he felt that great pain again. He lifted himself on his elbows and looked into his lap. Between the burnt pubic hair, above the hairy scrotum, was something black that resembled a heavily charred twig of a Christmas tree. A feeling of pure despair flooded him.

Then his gaze dropped to the carpet. Next to him laid his wife's tsantsa, whose mouth was twisted into a triumphant smile.

ABOUT THE CONTRIBUTORS

Lenny Ka
She studied journalism at Palackého University in Olomouc and now makes a living writing. She worked in local media, 21. Století magazine, and Czech television. Currently working for websites focused on economics and taxes. She published short stories at Děti noci website, in a small anthology of disturbing stories called Trash vol. 3., the art revue Pandora, and Howard magazine, to which she also contributes with articles and reviews.

Roman Vojkůvka
Writer, screenwriter, director. He has made several short films and featured low-budget horror films (Někdo tam dole mě má rád, Total Detox, Eskort, Příbuzenstvo) and feature-length documentary about Zora Ulla Kesler, the Czech actress known for starring in numerous Italian exploitation thrillers and horror movies. In 2014, his screenplay Na druhý pohled (At Second Glance) was adapted into a television film; in 2021, a feature adaptation of his screenplay Chyby (Mistakes) is being prepared for cinemas. He was the editor of Filmag extra, a magazine dedicated to horror movies. At the end of 2011, he published a collection of horror short stories Řezničina. In 2018 he published his existential novel Chránit pevnost.

Petr Boček
Archivist and historian by profession, writer by passion. In collaboration with Miloslav Zubík, he wrote 3 horror stories collections (Mrazivé povídky, Výprodej nočních můr, Nekrosarium). He also

contributed to various horror anthologies and published horror novels Hrobořadí and Mízožravci. His writing is a combination of rough horror and a dark humour. He is an editor of Howard magazine.

Miroslav Pech

He changed various jobs, currently anchored on the railway. Author of several existentially tuned books, including ironic humour in the form of short stories collections (Napíšu Pavle, Američané jedí kaktusy, Ohromně vtipná videa atd.) or novels (Cobainovi žáci, Otec u porodu). He made a debut in his favourite horror genre in 2018 with Mainstream, which is a raw and realistic story about marital breakdown. The novel was published in Poland first and only then in the Czech Republic, supplemented with several short stories. Pech also published his horror stories in several magazines and anthologies. Last year, he published the horror novel Dítě tmy (2020), and with Honza Vojtíšek, they published their novellas in a book Milenci ze snů/S meluzínou sůl lízat. His work is manifested in austerity and verbal minimalism.

Honza Vojtíšek

The Czech horror writer and editor. He works on railway. He is a publisher of horror e-magazine Howard. He edited couple of anthologies, he is organizing horror cons, and gives lectures about horror at cons and festivals. He published two books of short stories, the anthology Sešívance (Stitchers, 2018) contains stories where Honza is co-writer for all of them, other co-writers are from the Czech Republic, Slovakia, and Poland. His first novel is Kazatel (Preacher, 2019). In 2020, he published next anthology with his stories and stories by Ondřej Kocáb; he published book with two novels, one by him, the other by Miroslav Pech. His short stories were published in Slovak, Polish, and English. He wrote scripts to nine short comics, four of his stories were made into short movies. He loves horror, books, and eccentric music.

Martin Štefko

Czech author and publisher (Golden Dog). As a publisher, he is focusing on horror genre and has Czech, American, and Finnish authors in his portfolio. As an author, his genre spread is wider and he jumps from horror to action sci-fi and western, then over to detective story and thriller back to horror.

Ondřej Kocáb

Born in Zlín. He started writing his first horror stories, which were relatively soon successful in literary competitions, during his study of biophysics at the Palacký University of Olomouc. He debuted with his short stories in 2019 in the anthology Dokud nás smrt nerozdělí. The next year, he was completing, together with Honza Vojtíšek, another split collection of short stories named Rozpolcení. Macho-man 3000 is his first story published abroad.

Edward Lee

Edward Lee is the author of over 50 horror, fantasy, and sci-fi books, and dozens of short stories. He has also had comic scripts published by DC Comics, Verotik Inc., and Cemetery Dance. A great number of his novels have been reprinted in Germany, Poland, Italy, Romania, Japan, and other countries. He is a Bram Stoker Award Nominee; his Lovecraftian novel INNSWICH HORROR won the 2010 Vincent Price Award for Best Foreign Book (Austria), his novel WHITE TRASH GOTHIC won the 2018 Splatterpunk

Award for Best Extreme Horror Novel, and in 2020 Lee won the Splatterpunk Lifetime Achievement Award. In 2009, the movie version of his novella HEADER was released by Synapse Films. He lives in Seminole, Florida.

Karolína Svěcená *(translator)*
Master of anthropology, English teacher, and book blogger based in Pilsen, Czech Republic. During her studies, she worked as a barista and now can't live without a cup of strong coffee. Due to the covid situation, she started teaching English and eventually translating to make a living. She's always late and struggles with deadlines all the time. Whenever her schedule allows, she writes book reviews for her blog Kaleidoskop šílenství (Kaleidoscope of madness) and contributes to an online horror magazine Howard.

Kateřina Cukrová *(translator)*
Born in 1996 in Uherské Hradiště. She graduated in the field of English philology and Dutch philology at Palacký University in Olomouc. During her studies, she had various translation opportunities, including the translation of two chapters from Dutch into Czech in the book *Spolu "alejí Evropy"—100 let nizozemsko-česko-slovenských vztahů* (Together in the "Alley of Europe"—100 years of Dutch-Czech-Slovak relations). Further, she wrote one chapter in Czech language in the book *Raději mrtvý než být otrokem—Dějiny fríské literatury* (Better dead than being a slave—History of Friesian literature) and in the same book, she also translated one chapter from Dutch into Czech. The translation of the short story *Macho-man 3000* is her first translation from Czech into English.

MORE FROM
MADNESS HEART PRESS

Body Horror Anthology
978-1386684350

Hallucinations Anthology
979-8598457054

You Will Be Consumed by Nikolas Robinson
978-1-7348937-7-9

Extinction Peak by Lucas Mangum
979-8689548654

Lightning Source UK Ltd.
Milton Keynes UK
UKHW021142130222
398608UK00008BA/240